"Wait till Sean hears his principal is here visiting Mom," Laura Williams heard her son say as he ran off.

Peter's chuckle drew her attention. "They are very—lively. I'm sorry if I made the situation worse."

"You could have said you came here for my son."

"If I'm totally being honest, bringing his work was just an excuse. I really did come to see you."

Laura sucked in a deep breath. "You did?"

Again his intense gaze drilled into her. Heat spread across her cheeks. For a moment she forgot about the four kids in the house. Across the few feet that separated them a connection sprang up as if that meeting in his office had forged a link that already went beyond her son.

Books by Margaret Daley

MARGARET DALEY

feels she has been blessed. She has been married more than thirty years to her husband, Mike, whom she met in college. He is a terrific support and her best friend. They have one son, Shaun.

Margaret has been writing for many years and loves to tell a story. When she was a little girl, she would play with her dolls and make up stories about their lives. Now she writes these stories down. She especially enjoys weaving stories about families and how faith in God can sustain a person when things get tough. When she isn't writing, she is fortunate to be a teacher for students with special needs. Margaret has taught for over twenty years and loves working with her students. She has also been a Special Olympics coach and has participated in many sports with her students.

Once Upon a Family
Margaret Daley

Steeple
Hill®

Published by Steeple Hill Books™

STEEPLE HILL BOOKS

Steeple
Hill®

ISBN-13: 978-0-373-87429-3
ISBN-10:   0-373-87429-4

ONCE UPON A FAMILY

Copyright © 2007 by Margaret Daley

Printed in U.S.A.

Blessed be the God and Father of our
Lord Jesus Christ, the Father of mercies and God
of all comfort, who comforts us in all our
tribulations, that we may be able to comfort
those who are in any trouble, with the comfort
with which we ourselves are comforted by God.
—*2 Corinthians* 1:3-4

To Ashley and Alexa, you are precious and loved.

Chapter One

Laura Williams had never once, when she was a girl in school, been sent to see the principal. Today, she was standing in front of her son's Cimarron High principal's door. They'd only been in town for two weeks, and her oldest was already in trouble. Probably some kind of record. Her hand shook as she knocked.

When the door opened, she took a small step back. The tall, broad principal filled the entrance to his office. Her mouth went dry. With her small, just-over-five-feet stature his large presence overwhelmed her.

"Laura Williams?"

She swallowed hard, drew in a deep breath and stuck out her hand. "Yes. You must be Peter Stone."

His fingers closed around hers, a warm, firm grip. "Come in. I'm sorry we're meeting for the first time under these circumstances." He moved to the side to let her enter. "I wanted to talk with you alone before I bring Sean back in." He closed the door and rounded his massive desk, gesturing toward a chair in front of it. "Please have a seat."

"I can't believe Sean was fighting. He's never done anything like that before."

The principal flipped open a file and scanned a paper he'd picked up. "I see you all moved here a couple of weeks ago. How did Sean feel about the move?"

She looked into the man's dark brown eyes and saw kindness and concern. For a moment she wanted to tell him the whole story of how she and her four children had ended up in Cimarron City, Oklahoma. But the pain was still too fresh, and she didn't confide in many people, even one who gave off empathetic vibes. "We're adjusting."

Doubt entered his eyes. "When I asked Sean about the fight, he was silent. He hasn't said more than a sentence or two. I didn't know if the anger I was sensing from him went beyond the argument he had with the other boy."

"What was the argument about?" Laura clutched the handle of her zebra-striped purse tightly, her finger-nails and leather straps digging into her palms.

"The other boy told me Sean cheated off him in English."

"What did Sean say?"

"Nothing. I talked with his teacher and their test answers were remarkably similar."

Until recently her oldest had always been a good student. "Could the other boy have cheated off Sean?"

The principal frowned. "I don't think so. He's at the top of his class."

Dread blanketed her in a cold sweat. She'd hoped coming to Cimarron City would be a fresh start. "Who started the fight?"

"Your son."

Laura sat forward on the edge of the padded chair. "Are you suspending him?"

"That's our policy. Three days, until next Monday."

"Is the other student being suspended, too?"

He nodded.

She closed her eyes for a few seconds, thoughts of the hostility that was so much a part of her family since— No, she couldn't go there. That wouldn't change what was happening. She pushed to her feet. "Very well."

"Let me bring Sean in." He stood and walked to the door.

Laura faced her son as he trudged into the office, his eyes downcast. She didn't need to see them to know the defiance in their green depths. His clenched hands shouted his anger, always present since his father had passed away nine months ago.

The intense, churning emotions coming off the boy struck Peter with their force. The teen held his tall, thin frame in a rigid stance as though daring anyone to come near him. He was screaming for help. He'd seen the signs before. The anger. The silence. The defiance.

"Sean, as I said before, you'll be suspended for three days for fighting. When you come back, you'll retake the test." The tightening of the boy's mouth prompted Peter to add, "As will the other student, since we can't determine exactly who cheated. The test will be different, harder."

Laura stepped forward. "Thank you, Mr. Stone. He'll be prepared to take it." She waved her hand for her son to leave first. At the door she glanced back at him. "I appreciate the way you've handled the situation."

Peter watched the mother and son until they disappeared from his view. He turned back into his office, his gaze settling on the chair where Laura Williams sat only a few minutes ago. The haunted look in her green eyes tugged at his heart. A troubled soul.

And Sean was a troubled teen. He'd seen all the signs because he had been one himself years ago. If truth be told, he still felt—unsettled. He couldn't change what had happened, yet he couldn't quite put his past behind him. Peter strode to his desk and sat. The best way to help himself was to help someone else.

Seeing the pain in Laura and Sean Williams confirmed in Peter's mind what he should do. For the past six months he couldn't shake the feeling that the Lord wanted him to do more with his life. Being the principal of the high school and being involved in his church as a deacon weren't enough. God wanted something else from him. He picked up the phone and placed a call.

Laura unlocked the door to her side of the large duplex and tossed her purse on the entry hall table while Sean stomped up the stairs. On the drive home from school, her son had only mumbled a "yeah" to the question, "Do you understand you're grounded until you go back to school?"

The sound of Sean's bedroom door slamming vibrated in the air. Half the town probably heard that, especially Aunt Sarah. Thinking about the occupant of the other side of the duplex turned Laura around. She hadn't had a chance to check on her aunt this morning. She went out onto the long front porch they shared and walked the few feet to her aunt's. She let herself in and made her way through the small living room, crammed with years of items from Aunt Sarah's world travels, to the back where she usually was at this time of the day, drinking her third or fourth cup of tea and nibbling on what little she ate for a late breakfast.

"Child, what's going on over at your house? Is everything all right?" The seventy-nine-year-old woman with salt-and-pepper hair pulled back in a severe bun, put her china cup on its saucer.

Nothing was all right, but Laura didn't want to burden her aunt with any more of her problems. "That was just Sean. I had to pick him up from school."

With a trembling hand, Aunt Sarah held up a plate with several scones. "Want one? I don't know why I fixed both of these. I can hardly eat one."

Her stomach in knots, Laura shook her head and sank into the chair across from her aunt at the table for two in front of the bay window that looked out over the large backyard.

"Is Sean sick?"

"No." Laura slid her gaze away from Aunt Sarah's perceptive one.

"We're family. I was a teacher once. A student went home during the day for two reasons. He was sick or had gotten in trouble. What happened?"

The firmness in the woman's voice belied her frail appearance. Laura's gaze reconnected with her aunt's sharp, assessing one, her dark eyes in striking contrast to the pale cast of her skin. "Sean got into a fight at school and was suspended."

"Oh, my." She brought her cup to her lips and sipped. "I've been praying that he would adjust to his new home. It looks like I'd better continue."

What good was praying? Laura peered away, not wanting her aunt to see the conflict in her eyes. Aunt Sarah was a devout Christian who wouldn't understand the confusion she felt. She'd prayed for the past year, and God had ignored her pleas. Now she was having to accept charity from her aunt just to make ends meet and be able to take care of Sean, Alexa, and the twins—Matthew and Joshua. She didn't want to be indebted to anyone, even family, after spending so many years of her marriage feeling dependent—almost helpless in her situation.

Laura's gaze fastened on to the slightly overgrown backyard with leaves still strewn over the ground from last fall. "I'm gonna have Sean start working on the yard while he's home. I want to keep him busy." *So he doesn't spend all his time sulking in his bedroom. He's done too much of that lately.*

Her aunt looked out the window. "I've kind of let things go since my illness. This time of year is so beautiful. I love working in the garden in the spring and don't like that I can't."

"Just tell me what you want done, and Sean and I will do it."

"Well, thank you, dear, but you don't have to."

"I want to." Again Aunt Sarah's sharp gaze fell on her, her head held high, her posture straight. Her aunt had always appeared as though she could do anything, and while growing up she'd wanted to be just like Aunt Sarah, independent, confident, strong. For a few seconds Laura wondered just how ill her aunt was. *Had she really needed my help?* One moment she seemed delicate, easily broken, the next she seemed capable of battling the world.

Then the older woman's shoulders sagged and a deep sigh drifted from her. "I've got to get used to the fact I can't do everything I used to."

That can't be easy for her to admit, Laura thought.

Aunt Sarah sighed. "I'll make a list for you."

"And speaking of lists, I'll be going to the grocery store later. Just jot down what you need and I'll get it." Although she was living in the other side of the duplex rent free, she was determined to do everything she could to help Aunt Sarah. She was the reason Laura had uprooted her family and moved here after her aunt had triple bypass surgery. Who was she kidding? She hadn't been able to pay her debts living in St. Louis. Her aunt's invitation had been the answer to her problems after she had gotten the eviction notice.

"That's sweet of you. Before too long I'll be able to go with you to shop for myself. Each day I feel stronger and stronger." Aunt Sarah reached across the table and patted Laura's hand. "I'm so glad you and your children are here. Our family is a small one. We've got to stick together."

"We appreciated the invitation to live next door."

"Since my tenants moved out in January, it's been empty. It's ridiculous for the duplex to remain that way when you all could use it. You're doing me a favor by living in it."

"Just as soon as I can, I want to pay you rent."

"No! I won't accept it from family. End of story." Her aunt's mouth set in a stubborn line.

"But don't you need the money?"

She shook her head. "Money isn't important. Family is."

Laura agreed with her aunt, and yet the lack of money was causing all kinds of problems in her life. "I want to pay my own way. That's what you've done all your life. You've stood on your own two feet. I'm thirty-five. It's about time I learn how."

"Everyone needs help from time to time, even me." She waved a hand down her thin body, clad in her gown and robe. "Have you started job hunting yet?"

Relieved by the change in the topic of conversation, Laura looked at the plate of scones, her hunger now bubbling to the surface. "I've been scanning the paper the last couple of days, but everything requires skills I don't have." She'd learned that while looking for a decent job in St. Louis and having to settle for a temporary, low-paying one. "Now if someone wanted a mommy, I'd be perfect for that job. Or a housekeeper. Or a chauffeur."

"You're pretty good with the computer. Didn't you keep your husband's books the first few years of your marriage?"

After the business had started making money, her husband hadn't wanted her to work there anymore. "Yeah, but I don't have any formal bookkeeping training." Laura eyed the scone again, her stomach rumbling now.

"Go ahead. If I know you, you didn't eat much for breakfast. I heard you moving around unpacking right after the kids left for school."

Laura lathered butter and strawberry jam on the scone. "I only have a few more boxes to empty and I'll be completely finished. Hey, I could work for a moving company."

"I talked with my friend in the counseling office at the high school this morning. She's always checking on how I'm doing. She said they're looking for a part-time secretary. Why not apply for that job until something better comes along?"

After the meeting with the principal an hour ago, Laura had her doubts she could get the job. But the prospect of working at Sean's school appealed to her. That way she could keep an eye on him and maybe prevent something like today happening again. "I'll think about it."

"You're good with people. You'll be off when your kids are. It's twenty-five hours a week with health insurance and a few benefits."

"I can't do anything until Sean goes back to school on Monday."

"Child, he's fifteen."

"And I don't know if I can trust him to do what he's supposed to do." *Like father, like son.* She shivered with that thought.

"I can keep an eye on him."

"No," Laura said with more force than intended. "You're still recovering and don't need the added stress of keeping him in line."

"Sean and I get along just fine."

It was she and Sean who didn't get along. Laura didn't want to be reminded of that fact. Ever since her husband had died, her son had been angry at the world but mostly at her.

"If I'm meant to have the job, it'll be there next week when Sean goes back to school." Laura pushed herself to her feet and took the empty plate to the sink.

"Do you want me to make a call? I know it's been fourteen years since I retired, but I still know quite a few people who work for the school since I was a teacher there. Many of them go to my church."

Laura had to swallow the yes before she blurted it out. She needed to begin standing on her own two feet, like her aunt had all her life. She could no longer accept help if she was going to be able to face herself in the mirror each morning. She was tired of depending on others. "I've got it, Aunt Sarah. But thanks for the offer."

Her aunt pinched her lips into a frown but didn't say anything. She finished her tea while writing the list of groceries she needed.

Laura washed the dishes and put them in the draining rack, then wiped the counter. When she heard the sound of the paper being ripped off the pad, she turned toward Aunt Sarah, intending to take the list and leave before she gave in to the offer of assistance. It would be so easy to let others do for her, but she couldn't anymore. If she got the job at the school, it wouldn't be because her aunt made a call.

Aunt Sarah's long thin hand clutched the paper and

wouldn't let it go. "It's okay to accept help, child, especially the Lord's."

Laura snatched the list and hurried toward the door, mumbling, "I'll be back in a few hours with the food."

Outside on the porch she took a deep, calming breath of the cool spring air. A light breeze teased the stray strands of her ponytail. The promise of a beautiful day did nothing to lift her spirits. The sudden blare of her son's radio disturbed the quiet of the street.

With a heavy sigh, she headed into her duplex to switch off the music and put her son to work. With each step, she mentally prepared herself to do battle.

"Guess what, Mom? I met a girl today who's had part of her brain removed!" Laura's twelve-year-old daughter stacked the last glass from dinner in the dishwasher and closed it.

"She did? Why?" Laura washed the sink out then hung up the dishcloth.

"Mindy had seizures and it took care of them. She lives on a ranch and rides all the time. I want to learn to ride a horse. Can I take lessons?"

Thinking of all the bills she had to pay, Laura shook her head. The children's Social Security benefits only went so far. "Alexa, I don't have the money for that. I wish—"

"Ah, Mom, we never get to do anything anymore. Everything has changed."

"Now that I've got the house in order, I'll be looking for a job. Hopefully I'll have some money for things like that."

"In St. Louis we used to be able to do things. Go places. Daddy always made sure of it."

Laura's heart cracked. Her throat thickened. She refused to shed another tear.

"Why did he have to die?" With her eyes glistening, Alexa pressed herself against Laura.

The words hurt. An explanation lodged in her throat, but she'd decided that her children needed to be protected from the truth if possible. She didn't want to disillusion them about their father and yet—

Chimes resonated through the house.

Alexa pulled back, swiping the tears from her face. "That might be Hailey. She lives across the street." She rushed from the kitchen.

Watching her daughter leave swelled the ache ever present in Laura. How could she tell her children about the debt they were in because their father had gambled everything away? They had already lost the only home they had known. They'd had to move to another town and leave all their friends behind. She didn't want them to know what kind of man their father had become before he died.

"Mom, someone's here to see you."

Her daughter's shout pulled Laura away from the thoughts that had been hounding her for the past nine months. She hurried into the foyer and spied Peter Stone standing on the other side of the screen door. As Alexa headed up the stairs, Laura pasted a smile on her face and let Sean's principal into the house.

"Is something else wrong?" she asked, noting how the large man filled her small entry hall. He dominated the space around him and commanded attention, reminding her of the first glimpse she had of him in his office earlier that day.

His face lit with a grin, laugh lines fanning out from his dark, dark brown eyes. "No. I just thought I'd bring your son his work that he'll miss over the next couple of days. He might as well do it while he's home." He held up a stack of papers in a folder.

"Oh—" she gestured toward the living room "—I appreciate that. Come in and sit down. Would you like something to drink? I've got decaf coffee, tea, sodas."

He folded his long length onto the couch and placed Sean's work on the table before him. "No, thanks. I can't stay long. I still have some chores to do at the ranch."

Laura sat across from him. "You own a ranch?" She thought of the fact that she and her daughter had just been discussing Alexa's desire to learn to ride horses.

"Yep. A dream I had since I was a kid."

"Do you raise cattle?"

"No." His smile encompassed his whole face with dimples appearing in his cheeks and a gleam in his eyes. "I've only had the place a few years. It was pretty run-down so it's taken me a while to fix it up. I have some horses, though."

"Horses?" Again she was reminded of her daughter. If only—

"Yeah. I have five as well as other assorted animals that have been abandoned or rescued."

"You rescue animals?"

"When you live outside of town, some people think

it's okay to dump their pets on the side of the road. I guess they figure they'll fend for themselves out in the countryside. The sad truth is they often don't." Peter leaned forward and rested his elbows on his thighs, his fingers laced together.

"Do you find homes for them?"

"Sometimes." His intense gaze caught hers. "Are you looking for a pet?"

"Our dog died a few months back. My kids have been wanting another one, but since I knew I was moving, I told them we needed to wait."

One corner of his mouth tilted up. "Then I've got just the puppy for you."

Her pulse skipped a beat at his heart-melting smile, definitely his best asset even though his other features formed a pleasing picture. His medium brown hair held streaks of gold. His complexion, tanned obviously from spending time outdoors, had just begun to show a five o'clock shadow. She could visualize him riding a horse, a Stetson pulled down low to shadow those eyes that held an intensity in them, as though they could probe a person's innermost thoughts. "How young a puppy?"

"I'm guessing about three or four months."

"A mutt?"

"Part black Lab and part something I can't tell."

"Then he'll be a big dog."

"He's a she and yes, she'll be a good size. I only mentioned the puppy because I know Sarah has a big backyard with a fence."

"You know my aunt?" Sounds of footsteps pounding

down the stairs echoed through the house. Laura turned her attention toward the entrance.

"Mom, Matthew's cheating again." Joshua, the older of her seven-year-old twins by a whole nine minutes, rushed into the room with his brother on his tail.

"No, I'm not. He's lying again. I won the game fair and square. He's a sore loser." Her other seven-year-old glared at his twin.

"Just in case you two didn't notice, we have a visitor. Joshua, Matthew, this is Sean's principal, Mr. Stone."

Both boys' green eyes grew round while Matthew said, "We knew he was in *big* trouble."

"Yeah, what did he do now?" With bright red hair spiked on top and freckles sprinkled across his face, Joshua approached Peter. "He's always getting into trouble."

"I'm here to visit with your mother."

Peter's words stunned Laura. Her eyes grew as round as her sons'.

"If Sean's not in trouble, then why is his door closed?" Matthew joined his brother at his side.

"And he didn't say anything at dinner, either." Joshua nodded once as though that validated in his mind that Sean had done something wrong.

Still grappling with the fact that Peter Stone had said he had come to see her, Laura didn't respond. Peter shrugged and answered the twins, "Beats me."

As if suddenly bored with the conversation, both boys spun on their heels and raced from the room, but not before Laura heard Joshua say, "Wait till Sean hears his principal is here visiting Mom."

The sound of sneakers pounding up the stairs faded as the twins headed for Sean's bedroom and started pounding on his door. Her oldest yelled at his brothers to get lost.

Peter's chuckle drew her attention. "You have your hands full. They are very…lively."

She laughed. "Among other things. I've gotten a few gray hairs because of them."

"I'm sorry if I made the situation worse."

"You could have said you came here for Sean. They'll find out soon enough that he's suspended and why."

"It's not my place to say anything about what Sean did at school." Peter sat on the edge of the couch, his gaze fixed on the stack of papers on the table before him. "Besides, if I'm being totally honest, bringing his work was just an excuse. I really did come to see you."

Laura sucked in a deep breath, held it until her lungs burned, then slowly released it. "You did? Why?"

"Since you're new in town, I figured you didn't know very many people and our meeting this morning in my office wasn't any way to greet a newcomer."

Again his intense gaze drilled into her. Heat spread across her cheeks. For a moment she forgot about the four kids in the house. Across the few feet that separated them a connection sprang up as if that meeting in his office had forged a link that already went beyond her son. Laura wished she could deny the response she felt, but she couldn't. She began to wonder if her hair was neat, her clothes not too wrinkled.

His mouth hitched into a half grin that did funny

things to her stomach. The kindness and concern she'd glimpsed earlier filled his expression. "Your Aunt Sarah and I go way back. She's a special lady I'd do anything for."

She latched onto his words and focused her attention on them rather than the way he made her feel. "That's the second time you've referred to my aunt. You know her well then? She's been retired for fourteen years so I doubt you two worked together."

"She was my high school algebra teacher."

"And now you're the principal of that high school."

He chuckled. "Which has surprised a few people."

"Oh, why?"

"Let's just say I knew the inside of my office intimately before I became principal." His grin disappeared and a serious look descended on his chiseled features. "That's why I can identify with your son. I was a very angry young man when I was his age."

Chapter Two

Shock widened Laura's beautiful green eyes and her mouth dropped open. She pressed her full lips together and slid her gaze to the side for a moment before reestablishing eye contact. "Then you give me hope that Sean will get through this and do something wonderful with his life."

Peter thought about his impulse to drop by the Williams's home and was no longer surprised by it. *Lord, is this what you want me to do?* For months a restlessness had taken hold of him. He'd felt as though he needed to do more for the students at his school. Today he'd been touched by Sean's plight. He normally didn't handle the discipline at Cimarron High. That job usually fell to his assistant principal, but since he was out of town at a conference, Peter had stepped in.

"I won't kid you. It wasn't easy for me. I fought it every step of the way, but I had foster parents who cared and teachers like Sarah. They didn't give up on me."

Laura straightened her petite frame, her shoulders squared. "And I won't give up on my son."

"I didn't think you would, but sometimes you need help. I could talk to Sean if you want. Before I was the principal, I was the head counselor."

"At his old school, he met several times with his counselor. It didn't help. In fact, he got angrier. He refused to talk to me for days because I pushed him to go see her."

"Why is he so angry?"

Laura stiffened, gripping her hands together in her lap. "It really came out when my husband…died. Sean was having a difficult time before that, but he became hostile after Stephen passed away."

"I'm so sorry about your husband. The death of a parent can be hard on any child." He knew from personal experience just how hard.

"I think it's more than that, but I don't know what. He won't say. I suppose it could be hormones. This age can be difficult."

Anxiety emanated from her. Suddenly, Peter felt like wrapping his arms around her to comfort her. Stunned by the feeling of connection, Peter recited to himself all the reasons why getting involved with Laura wouldn't work. But even remembering his failed marriage didn't suppress the feeling that, with the Lord's blessing, there could be more between them. "Perhaps I could become involved less formally. Not as his principal. Your Aunt Sarah goes to the same church as I do and the youth group—"

"I haven't decided about going to church or not." A closed expression instantly covered Laura's pretty features.

"I'm sure there's another way then. Let me think on it."

"Why?"

"Why do I want to help?"

She nodded, her stress showing in the white-knuckle clasp of her hands.

"Someone helped me once. I want to return the favor. Paul Henderson, my foster father, died last year. I owe him."

Pain edged its way into her eyes. "I'm sorry for your loss." Laura rose. "I know you've got chores to do, and I don't want to keep you. Thanks for bringing Sean's work. I'll make sure he does it while he's home." A polite mask pushed the pain from her expression, but the hands at her sides trembled slightly.

Her vulnerability beckoned him even though warning bells sounded in his mind. He had no business trying to help a wounded soul. He couldn't fix himself, let alone someone else. *Why me, Lord?*

Peter came to his feet and took a step toward her, but her rigid stance stopped him, as though she had closed a door and put up a Do Not Disturb sign. "How about the puppy? Want to come out to the ranch on Saturday and take a look at her? Bring the whole family. I'll give you the grand tour, such as it is."

Again she averted her gaze, lost in thought for what seemed interminably long seconds. Then she inhaled deeply, as if fortifying herself, and looked at him. "That would be nice. My daughter, Alexa, loves horses."

"The young lady who answered the door?"

"Yes, she's twelve and crazy about them. Just today she was talking about learning to—" She halted abruptly as though surprised at what she was saying. She offered him a smile and started for the front door. "What time would be good for you? I don't want to inconvenience you."

"How about ten?"

"Where's your ranch?"

"Only a mile outside of town on the left hand side of Highway 101. There's a sign at the gate. Stone's Refuge." He made his way to the foyer. "I figured if I was taking in all those animals I might as well call it what it is." In more ways than one, but he kept that thought to himself. Taking care of the animals and riding over his land were his escape from the day-to-day stresses, from the memories.

She opened her front door and moved out onto the porch. "I like the name."

"I hope you'll bring Sean, too."

"Is this your roundabout way to try to help my son?"

There was a light tone to her voice now, even though her expression was hidden from him in the evening shadows. He moved toward the stairs. "It's hard to resist an animal in need of love."

The sound of her quick indrawn breath followed him to his Chevy truck. He glanced back and waved. Although Laura still stood in the shadows, he felt her gaze on him. He could still picture her red hair with brown woven through it and the striking green eyes. Clear. Perceptive. Windows into a wounded soul. His earlier assessment of Laura Williams had been affirmed by this meeting. She was in need of a friend. He just didn't know if he should be that friend.

* * *

Peter Stone's large, black, four-door truck pulled away from the curb. Laura stayed still, her attention fixed on the disappearing taillights. When he turned the corner and was gone from sight, she walked the few feet to her aunt's and let herself in.

"Aunt Sarah," she called out and crossed to the hall that led to the back.

"In the kitchen."

When she entered the room, her aunt, dressed in one of her flannel gowns and a blue terry cloth robe shuffled from the counter to the table, carrying the hot milk that she drank right before bedtime.

"Tell me what you know about Peter Stone." Laura took the chair across from the older woman.

Aunt Sarah brought the mug to her lips and took a tentative sip. "So that was who I heard you talking to on the porch." She put the mug on the flowered place mat. "I guess you know he's the principal of the high school. Is he the one who suspended Sean this morning?"

"Yes, he brought over Sean's schoolwork."

"That was nice of him, but then I'm not surprised. He does those kinds of things all the time. A hard worker. A respected member of the community. He's always going out of his way to help someone."

"He mentioned something about being in trouble as a teenager."

"Yes, he was quite a handful at one time."

"What did he do?"

Aunt Sarah chuckled. "I'll let him tell you about

some of the…pranks he pulled." She drank some more of her milk. "But I will tell you that he would be perfect to relate to Sean."

"That's what he said."

"He did? Wonderful. If he's offered to help, take him up on it. A man in Sean's life might be just what the boy needs."

Laura clenched her teeth to keep from saying she didn't need a man in their lives. A man was the reason they were in the situation they were in at the moment. In debt. Hurting. Adrift.

Laura rose, leaned down and kissed her aunt on the cheek. "Is there anything you want me to do before I go?"

"No, I'm going to finish this milk and go to bed. Maybe tomorrow I'll come out and help you and Sean work on the flower beds."

Laura rested her hand on her waist. "You'll take it easy until the doctor says you can. No working but you can come out and talk to us while we do."

Her aunt's humph echoed through the kitchen as Laura left. It was getting harder to persuade Aunt Sarah to rest and let Laura do for her. *But she's met her match. I can be just as determined.* She'd discovered that aspect of her personality during the past year.

When Laura opened the door to her duplex, Sean sat on the bottom stair, waiting for her. The second she entered he shot to his feet and covered the distance between them.

"What was *he* doing here?" Anger manifested itself in her son's surly expression.

"Do you mean your principal?"

"Yes!"

"He brought your schoolwork for you to do."

Sean crossed his arms over his chest and glared at her. "I know what we're doing in class. I didn't need him to do that."

"Well, he thought he needed to." Laura started walking toward the back where her bedroom was. "I think it's nice that he cared enough to stop by."

"Joshua said he came to see you."

The accusation in her son's eyes cut through her. She stopped at the door into her bedroom, formally the den, and faced him. "Yes, he did. He has a puppy we can have. We're going out to his ranch on Saturday to see if the puppy is what we want. I expect you to go. This will be a family decision."

"I'm busy."

"Doing what? You're grounded until you go back to school. You're going." Laura slipped into her room before her son drew her into an argument. She didn't have the energy left to debate with Sean tonight.

She walked to her desk, sank onto the chair and switched on her old computer. She'd promised Cara, her best friend in St. Louis, she'd e-mail her to let her know she'd settled in and to give Cara her new phone number. She'd been putting it off because she was afraid she would pour her heart out to Cara. She'd even ignored a couple of e-mails, but she couldn't any longer. Maybe telling her about Peter Stone was just what she needed to put her feelings for the man in perspective.

Saturday morning, Laura glanced at Sean, sitting in the front seat of her red Escort with his arms folded across his chest and a glare on his face. He wasn't happy about coming to Stone's Refuge and had been vocal in his protest. It was only a few minutes to ten and already she was exhausted from battling her oldest child and getting the other three ready and organized for this little outing. If she hadn't promised her kids a new dog when they came to Cimarron City, it would have been easier to stay home and forget the principal's offer.

But forget Peter Stone? Not possible, especially after her thoughts for the past few days had been invaded by the man's presence. Not even e-mailing Cara had worked. She'd actually bounded out of bed, looking forward to this outing.

"There it is!" Alexa pointed to a large arch with the name of the ranch done in wrought iron letters over the entrance.

Laura turned onto the gravel road with brown wooden fences running down both sides. Two tan horses grazed on one side while another with a gray coat was in the pasture to the left. At the end sat a brown barn, the large doors in the center open wide as though welcoming them. Peter stood in the entrance watching the car approaching. A white cat weaved its body in and out between his legs, while a massive German shepherd sat beside him.

"Is that the dog?" Matthew asked, his eyes round.

"No, honey. We're here to look at a puppy." Hopefully one that when it was full grown would be a bit smaller than the German shepherd. She saw another dog dart across the field—another big one with shaggy hair.

The second Laura cut the engine, the twins flung the doors open and charged across the yard toward the barn.

The dog next to Peter stood up, his ears perked forward. Joshua came to a skidding halt when he saw the big dog rise. Matthew collided right into Joshua, sending him flying forward to land sprawled at Peter's feet. Matthew froze, his attention riveted on the German shepherd.

"Bosco, sit." Peter helped Joshua up. "He won't hurt you. He really is a big baby. All my dogs are."

"Big is the right word." Joshua backed up until he bumped into his twin.

"You two are stupid. You should never run toward any animal who doesn't know you like that." Sean laughed and walked toward the German shepherd at a sedate pace. He held out his hand and let the dog sniff him before petting him.

Peter grinned at Sean. "You're good with animals."

Her oldest son grumbled something under his breath and lowered his head, but he kept stroking the dog.

Peter motioned for the twins to come forward. They obeyed at a much slower rate and mimicked their brother's greeting with Bosco. The dog's tail wagged, and he licked Matthew's hand.

"That tickles." Matthew giggled and ran his palm along Bosco's back.

Laura observed the scene and knew it was a good decision to get another dog.

Joining her three brothers, Alexa turned her attention to the white cat at Peter's feet. She picked it up and buried her face in its fur. "What's her name?"

"She's Molly." Peter moved toward Laura while keeping an eye on the children with Bosco. "Did you have trouble finding the ranch?"

"Nope. Your directions were great." She turned in a full circle, gesturing around her. "I really like your place. If you bought this run-down, it's obvious you've put a lot of work into it."

"Most of my spare time these past few years has been spent at this ranch." Satisfaction curved his mouth upward and lit his eyes. "I've nearly gotten it how I want it."

"We need to do that with Aunt Sarah's duplexes. They need to be painted. The yard cleaned up. Some of the interior renovated."

"I've certainly developed the expertise since I bought the ranch. I've gotten quite good with a hammer, saw and a paintbrush. If you need any help, just let me know."

The word *why* almost slipped from her mouth. Then she remembered he was fond of her aunt and probably wanted to help Sarah. Laura shifted her gaze back toward her children. She really had no home anymore. This move to Cimarron City was a temporary one, at least where she presently lived, especially since her aunt refused to accept any rent. Aunt Sarah was retired and surely could use the money she would get from renting the other half of the house. Even though she had said she didn't care about the money, Laura wouldn't be responsible for her aunt not getting what she should have coming to her. As soon as she could get back on her feet financially, she would find her own place and take charge of her affairs completely.

"I will," Laura murmured, realizing Peter expected some kind of reply to his generous offer. But she couldn't see herself calling him up and inviting him over to paint the house.

"Do you all want to meet the puppy?" Peter strode toward her children still gathered around the two pets.

Joshua jumped to his feet. "Yes!"

Matthew and Alexa rose, too, her daughter finally putting the cat back on the ground. Molly immediately began rubbing against the girl's legs. The three began heading toward the barn right behind Peter when Sean whispered something into the German shepherd's ear then slowly got to his feet. His stance and expression spoke of his conflicting emotions. He wanted to see the puppy but didn't want anyone to know.

Laura settled her arm on Sean's shoulders. "This pet is for the whole family. I need everyone's approval. C'mon."

He shrugged away and plodded toward the entrance of the barn. Laura blew out a frustrated breath and followed, slowly counting to ten, then proceeding to twenty, then thirty. By the time she reached it, her tensed muscles relaxed and her resolve to enjoy this outing returned.

"Mom! She's so cute. Look." Matthew struggled to hold a squirming black-and-brown puppy against his chest.

"I want to hold her, too." Joshua tried to take the animal from his twin.

Before there was a tug-of-war with the twenty-pound puppy as the rope, Laura hurried forward. "Put her down. We have plenty of time for everyone to pet and love her."

"Hey, squirts, there are certain privileges to being the firstborn. One is I get to check her out before you guys." Sean marched past Laura and waded into the middle of the other three kids gathered around the dog.

Peter moved to her side. "I think she's a hit."

"I really had little doubt. My kids love animals. If I let them, we would have a whole houseful."

"Sorta like me."

She laughed. "Yep. I'll use you as an example and tell them when they grow up they can be just like you." She glanced at him, liking what she saw. He wore blue jeans, a plaid short-sleeved shirt and boots. All he needed to complete the picture of a cowboy was the Stetson she'd imagined him wearing the other day.

He snagged her gaze, his dark eyes bright. "Do you all want the grand tour?"

"I hate to take up too much of your time."

"I don't get to show off my ranch nearly enough after all the hard work I've put in."

"Well, in that case, yes." She swung her gaze to her children. "What do you all think? Do you want the puppy?"

A chorus of "yes" greeted her question.

"Great. Mr. Stone wants to show us around."

"Can we see the horses?" Alexa picked up the white cat that had followed her into the barn and held her against her chest.

"Sure. Your mom said something to me about how much you like horses. You ought to come out here and ride sometime."

Alexa's face split into a huge grin. "Yes! Can I today?"

"Alexa Dawn, you can't invite—"

"Mom, he said I could." Her daughter's gaze skipped to Peter. "I can come whenever you want."

The laugh lines deepened at the corner of Peter's eyes. "Tell you what. Why don't we have a tour then grab something to eat? After lunch you all can ride. That is, if it's okay with your mom."

Everyone looked at her. Laura thought about the four loads of laundry that still needed washing, the bathrooms that needed cleaning, the— But she couldn't say no when she peered at her oldest child and his usual frown wasn't in place. Granted he wasn't smiling, either, but his expression actually appeared almost pleasant for a change.

"You don't have to fix us lunch," she finally answered.

"It's turning out to be a gorgeous day, and for March we take every one we can get. I have some hot dogs. It would be fun to put them on the grill and eat on the patio. If it will make you feel better, you can help me throw something together."

"If you're sure, then I guess so—"

The shouts of joy that permeated the barn produced a laugh in Peter. "I'm sure. C'mon." His hand slipped casually to the small of her back as he indicated a stall and started toward it. "Our first stop is the mare who just gave birth two nights ago."

His light touch radiated warmth, reminding Laura of his effect on her. Surprise kept her by his side for a few seconds before she sidestepped away and turned back toward her oldest son.

"A foal!" Alexa rushed to keep up with Peter, Matthew and Joshua, right on their heels as they headed to the last stall in the barn.

Laura came to Sean's side. He stroked the puppy while he remained kneeling next to the animal. "Coming, honey?"

He shook his head. "Horses are Alexa's thing. I'm staying here with Lady."

"Lady?"

"Yep, I've decided that's her name." He turned his face up toward her, a challenge in his expression. "Alexa named Brownie."

"It's still a family decision." Laura braced herself for his anger.

He frowned. "I'm sure they'll agree." He averted his face and focused on the black-and-brown puppy playing at his side.

As she walked toward the others, her oldest son's tensed shoulders eased and a look of joy entered his expression as he interacted with the dog. Lady would be good for Sean. Hope glowed inside Laura for the first time in a long while.

"You don't have to clean up the dishes." Peter came inside from the backyard. "I invited you and your family to lunch."

"The least I can do is this." Laura rinsed out a glass and put it on the counter above the dishwasher.

She looked so at home standing before the sink in his kitchen. The impromptu lunch had been a great idea. Her children had wolfed down his whole supply of hot dogs and then spent most of their time playing with his various pets. One of their favorites was his ferret, Digger. "Then let me help." He took the dishes she was stacking and started putting them in the dishwasher.

"You know my kids are gonna want a ferret next, and it will be all your fault."

"Yeah, I wouldn't be surprised. I even saw Sean playing with him when he wasn't with Lady."

"I'm glad the others are going along with that name."

"I like it. I hadn't picked one out yet. I just got her last weekend."

"How?" Laura finished the last glass and wiped down the sink.

"The same way as the ferret. Someone placed them at my gate. Digger was in a cardboard box with a few holes in it and Lady was tied to the post by a leash."

"How long have you had Digger?"

"A year. He got the name when he kept digging up my houseplants." Peter gestured toward his living area. "Now I don't even bother with indoor plants. It was too much of a hassle."

"So you've ferret-proofed your house."

Peter laughed. "I hadn't thought of it that way, but you're right. I also had to do something about my electrical cords."

"When can we take Lady home?"

"Today is fine by me. I doubt the kids would let you leave without her."

"That's great. We can stop by the pet store on the way home and get all the stuff we'll need. I still have some of the things from our last dog so we don't need much." She peered out the window over the sink. Her twins played with Digger while Sean wrestled with Lady who thumped his chest with the large paws she would eventually grow into. Alexa sat on the step, cuddling Molly in her lap. "This is just what they needed, especially Sean."

The wistful tone in her voice underscored the vulnerability he'd glimpsed and touched a place he'd kept suppressed since his former wife had walked away from their eight-year marriage. "I'm glad to see he isn't giving me scowls anymore even if he did stay on the other side of the yard."

She faced him. "As I told you before, this past year has been hard on him. He didn't take his dad's death well at all, but he was angry even before his death." She shook her head. "You can tell I'm really worried. I don't usually tell strangers things like that."

"I'd hope we are past the stranger stage. After all, we just shared an intimate lunch with four kids."

The sound of her laughter wrapped around him and left a warm feeling in its wake. "You forgot the cat, three dogs, rabbit and ferret."

"Oh, yeah, and them, too." He got the feeling she hadn't laughed much lately. He closed the dishwasher and leaned against the counter. "I'm so glad I found a good home for Lady. It probably won't be long before I have another puppy at my front gate to replace her."

"Aren't you concerned that people seem to be leaving the animals purposely at your ranch?"

He raked his hand through his hair and lifted one

corner of his mouth up. "Word does seem to have gotten around that I take in strays."

"What's gonna happen when you run out of room?"

"Hopefully someone like you and your family will help me with that problem." He pointed toward the chairs at the old oak table in front of a large window that afforded a view of the backyard. After she settled across from him, he continued, "I've been thinking lately about that. I have the land to take care of a lot of abandoned animals, but I want to do more than that."

She tilted her head to the side, her forehead creased. "Like what?"

"When I named my ranch Stone's Refuge recently, it got me thinking. What if I have more than a refuge for animals? What if it was a place to help kids, too? You saw how Sean responded to Lady, and even Digger."

"Do you have the time? The means?"

"I deal with teens every day who are in trouble and left to fend for themselves. What if I gave them something to do that was worthwhile?"

Laura glanced outside at the twins playing with the ferret, Sean caring for Lady, and her daughter holding the cat. "Still, it could be time-consuming."

"Granted I would need help, but it could be done. I have two friends who, like me, have been looking for something to do." He thought of his foster brothers, Jacob Hartman and Noah Maxwell. Hardship and redemption had molded them into a family. "It's just in the planning stages up here—" he tapped his temple "—and summer will be here in no time at all."

"It's the first of March."

"The spring semester goes by so fast. Kids will be looking for something to do in the summer."

"Yeah, I'll have four to keep busy." She slanted a glance toward the window. "Hey, I've got four children you could keep busy this summer." Her eyebrows shot up. "I mean...I—"

He chuckled. "I may take you up on the offer if they're willing. Of course, I've got to decide what to do first."

"At least you've got a plan, of sorts."

Something in her voice made him ask, "And you don't have a plan?"

"I've finished putting the house in order. Now I need to find a job. I don't want to work full-time right now with my aunt still recovering and all that's going on with my children. I need to be at the house when they come home from school."

"What are you looking for?"

"That's just it. I've been home with the kids since I got married and have little work experience. As a teen I was a waitress and know I don't want to do that again. I know my way around a computer. I'm good at hustling kids to and fro. I love to cook. Hate to clean house but do a good job anyway." She gave him a small smile. "That's the extent of my talents."

"We've got a secretarial opening in the counseling office. We're still interviewing for it. If you're interested in it, you should apply."

"My aunt said something to me about it a few days ago. I didn't want to do anything until Sean went back to school."

"Come in Monday then and put in an application. We want to fill it before spring break in two weeks. I have to warn you, April will be hectic with state mandated testing."

"I live a hectic life. I have four kids." She rose. "Which reminds me, I should check on them."

"And I promised your family a chance to ride."

When Peter walked outside behind Laura, her daughter ran up to him with anticipation in her expression. "Are we gonna see the horses now and ride?"

Alexa's excitement reminded him of the power animals could have on a person. When they left today, he would call Jacob and Noah. He needed to do more than dream about the refuge. Laura's family had given him the jump start he needed to get moving on it.

Chapter Three

"How's working in the counseling office going for you?" Peter took the chair next to Laura in the high school auditorium.

"You didn't hear anything?" she blurted out, tired after the first day on the job, learning all the procedures and people's names. If it wasn't for Sean having to be at this fund-raising auction, she would be home, getting ready for bed early.

"Should I have?" His lips twitched as though he were fighting a smile. He couldn't contain it. A grin spread across his features. "Oh, you mean the third-hour bell."

"Okay, so I didn't have the schedule memorized and made a tiny little mistake."

Full-fledged laughter erupted from Peter. People around them glanced over. "The ladies in the cafeteria weren't too happy, but the students were ecstatic they got an extra ten minutes for lunch."

The heat of a blush seared her cheeks. "Thankfully

the bells usually don't have to be rung manually. I brought the schedule home to memorize so that won't happen again. I will say in my defense, you have the craziest class schedule, actually two schedules because of homeroom on Thursdays. Nothing is on the hour or half hour. Most of the times are like 9:43."

His mouth twitched again. "Besides the bell incident, everything else all right?"

"I really enjoyed the work. I met some nice people. Thanks."

"I didn't do a thing. You got the job on your own." He peered toward the stage as the Future Farmers of America's program started. "How's Sean feel about you working at the high school?"

"Let's just say he didn't cheer at the news and leave it at that." Her son's icy demeanor could have frozen the tropics. She still remembered his words that she just wanted to spy on him. As he had stormed away, she couldn't deny the words totally. She did want to keep an eye on her son, but the job was actually perfect for her. The hours. The duties. The people.

"Will he be up on the auction block tonight?"

"Yes. He grumbled that he didn't want to do it, but it's a requirement since he's an FFA member."

"It's one of their big fund-raisers. I always bid on several students. Helps the program and helps me around the ranch."

She'd promised her son she would bid on him, but she didn't have much money, especially after getting some supplies for Lady. They would be eating more peanut butter sandwiches the next few weeks, but in her heart she knew Sean was afraid no one would bid on him. He would never admit it, though. "He's the third one up."

The first student came out on stage. The auction began for the boy's service for an eight-hour day. Laura glanced around. The auditorium was full of parents and friends. She was glad it was a well-attended function, but she was worried, too. They were new in town, and Sean hadn't made any friends, had even antagonized several boys because of his attitude. All she had was twenty-five dollars and the first two students had gone for a lot more than that.

Her breath trapped in her lungs, she watched her son walk out onto the stage, his expression not exactly a frown but nothing inviting in it, either. She exhaled slowly and sat forward as the auctioneer began.

For a few seconds no one said anything. Laura lifted her hand, but before she could say, "Five dollars," Peter shouted out, "Thirty dollars."

Her son squinted, scanning the audience until he found who had bid on him. When he saw Peter next to her, his frown appeared.

"Are you sure?" she whispered.

"Yep. This is my roundabout way to get to know your son."

Someone raised his hand and said, "Thirty-five."

"Fifty," Peter countered immediately.

When the bidding war was over between Peter and a man with long dark hair pulled back with a leather strap, Sean went for eighty-five dollars and the teen's frown lifted briefly when the amount was announced.

"That's an awfully expensive roundabout way to get to know Sean. I could have just brought him over."

Peter smiled. "I know. But as I said I always get a couple of guys to help me with the spring cleaning around the ranch."

"I'd better warn you Sean isn't your most motivated worker. He's been cleaning up Aunt Sarah's yard and griping the whole time. I've learned to turn a deaf ear to it."

His eyes took on a gleam. "Then I'll have to do that, too." Peter peered toward the stage. "Oh, good. Brandon is another teen I want to bid on."

By the end of the event Peter had purchased the services of three boys and hurried up to the front of the auditorium to pay. Laura hung back as the group of FFA members came down off the stage and began to mingle with the crowd. Sean glanced around, found her and headed straight toward her. The look in his eyes made her stiffen as he stopped in front of her.

"Mom, how could you let *him* buy me?"

His raised voice drew several people's attention. She pulled him to the side, away from the others. "First, I told you I only had twenty-five dollars. Second, I can't control what Mr. Stone decides to do. It's only for eight hours."

"An eternity if you ask me."

Peter weaved his way through the crowd, coming straight for her and Sean. "You'll do it and you'll do a good job."

"Hi, Sean. I just spoke to Brandon. I'd like you all to work the Saturday after spring break. Okay?"

Her son glared at her, refusing to look toward Peter. "Yeah, fine."

His tone indicated there was nothing fine about the situation. Laura cringed, balling her hands at her side. "Sean, why don't you go on out to the car? I'll be along in a minute." Thankfully he didn't make a comment as he hurried away. "I'm sorry about that. As you can tell, he isn't too happy. I probably should come with him to make sure he does what he needs to."

Peter shook his head. "That would only make matters worse. We'll do okay. If I'm going to help him, I have to establish a relationship with him."

"I see it's been another successful auction." A man almost as large as Peter paused next to him. He smiled at Laura, his chocolate-brown eyes full of humor. "And I see you have captured the attention of the prettiest woman here tonight. I'm Jacob Hartman." He held out his hand.

Laura shook it. "I'm Laura Williams. It's nice to meet you."

The ponytailed man who had also bid on Sean approached and slapped Peter on the back. "Hi, Peter."

"Noah Maxwell, this is Laura Williams." Peter nodded toward her. "These two are the friends I told you about. I'm trying to persuade them to help with Stone's Refuge."

Noah winked. "We're just letting him think he has to talk us into it. We were sold the first time he mentioned it to us. Is he roping you into helping, too?"

"I'd like to. It's certainly needed." *Maybe Peter can reach my son since I've tried everything I can think of.*

Laura might want to do things on her own, but when it came to her children's well-being, she would do anything she had to.

"That's great." Noah flashed her a smile. "I was afraid all we would have to look at is his ugly mug."

Peter chuckled. "Ignore him, Laura. Noah prides himself on playing the field."

"There's nothing wrong with being a confirmed bachelor." Noah scanned the crowd. "Which reminds me. I need to find my date."

Jacob shook his head, disbelief in his expression. "You brought a date to the FFA auction, Big Spender! Are your restaurants going under?"

"Funny." Noah looked at Laura. "I own a chain of restaurants that make the best pizza in the state—actually, let's make that the Southwest, and—" he slid his gaze back to Jacob "—I don't take kindly to the fact you think I'm cheap. I have a date with Nancy, an English teacher at the high school who needed to come here first because she promised some of her students."

The laughter in the man's eyes belied his words of accusation. The camaraderie among the three was evident in their casual air and teasing tones. Laura missed her friends in St. Louis, especially Cara Winters. She felt so alone in the midst of the crowd.

"Why did you decide to come?" Peter asked Jacob.

"A couple of my patients wanted me to." Jacob lifted his shoulders in a shrug. "So I'm here. I'm painting the clinic so I decided to purchase a few teens to help me."

"Are you a doctor?" Laura didn't have one for her

children yet, and with her school employment she could now get insurance. It was another reason the job had been so attractive to her.

"He's the best pediatrician in Cimarron City," Peter answered for his friend.

Jacob chuckled. "I need to hire Peter. He's the best publicist I could have." His beeper went off. He checked it and added, "I've got to go. I'm on call. Nice to meet you, Laura."

"Ah, I see Nancy. She's finished paying for her student. See you both later." Noah made his way toward the front of the auditorium.

"How far along are you with your plans for Stone's Refuge?" Laura turned her attention to Peter, suddenly aware they were alone in the back, off to the side.

"Other than roping those two into helping, not far. Did you mean it when you said you wanted to help? I could use a woman's perspective since I want to reach both male and female students at risk. Our first meeting is this Saturday. Can you come?"

"When?"

"One."

"Sean'll be at school. He's working on a project for the FFA. I'll have to check and see if Alexa can stay with the twins."

"Tell you what. Bring them. Alexa can have her second riding lesson." Peter grinned. "Actually, why don't we all ride after the planning meeting? My horses need to be ridden, and I could tell Joshua and Matthew were interested when you came to get the puppy."

"You make it hard to say no."

"That's the point. I need help so I'm using everything at my disposal to persuade you. Is it working?"

His teasing produced a lightness in her that she'd missed the past few years. For a brief moment she had forgotten all her worries. "Yes."

"So the lady you were with the other night at the auction is coming out here today to help us plan. Interesting. Do you have something to tell us?" Jacob took his seat at the dining room table in Peter's house.

Peter grinned. "I thought it was nice of her to want to help."

"I'm sure you did." Noah came in from the kitchen and placed his mug on a notepad.

Peter's grip around his cup tightened. "Let's get one thing straight before Laura comes. We are only friends. And we haven't even been friends for long. So quit trying to make something out of nothing."

"I do believe you're protesting too much. How many kids did you say she had?" Jacob asked with a chuckle.

"Four."

"Ah." Jacob lifted his mug to his lips to hide his smirk, but he wasn't successful in masking his amusement.

Peter narrowed his gaze on his so-called friend. "What's that supposed to mean?"

"I just find it interesting."

"Quit saying that word." Peter wanted to chalk up his irritable mood to the fact he hadn't slept for the past few nights. Plans for the refuge swirled around in his mind—along with images of Laura. But he knew what his foster brother was getting at. "I'm the oldest. I should get some respect for that." He glanced at his watch. *She's late.*

Noah slipped into a chair. "Sure, you're nine months older than me and six with Jacob. That's probably given you tons more wisdom."

"Have you met all her children?" Jacob finally drank some of his coffee.

"Yes."

"And her oldest son is in trouble?"

Jacob's persistence reminded Peter of a pit bull he'd once taken in until he'd found it a home. "I don't think Sean's adjusting well to his father's death or the move to Cimarron City."

"Interesting."

Peter brought the flat of his hand down on the table. "Stop right now. Yes, she has children. Yes, I always wanted to be a father. But there's no correlation between those two facts."

"I think she sure is pretty." Noah relaxed back in his chair.

Peter frowned. "And don't forget you're dating Nancy right now. Or is that over already?"

"Ouch!" Noah thumped his chest. "You wound me. I know better than to date a woman with a child, let alone children. I'm not like you. I don't want to be a father. Don't forget I've seen the bad side of fatherhood."

Jacob nodded. "I did, too, but that won't stop me when I meet the right woman. I want to have children. But this discussion isn't about us. It's about Peter and the new lady in town."

"We have better things to do than plan my love life." Peter reached for a pad, needing to steer the conversation in another direction before he said something he would regret. He would love to be a father, but he couldn't see himself marrying again. Not after Diana.

"What love life? When Diana walked out on your marriage, she took your love life with her."

"That's an *interesting* way to phrase what Diana did." Anger toward his ex-wife still festered in Peter's heart, especially when he remembered, which he made a point of not doing. So why now?

After three years he wished he could say he was finally over Diana's betrayal, but he wasn't. Having another man's child wasn't something he could easily forget, not when he saw her from time to time with her new husband and two children. He never wanted to go down that path again, put himself in a position to be hurt like that once more.

"It's so much easier to date a different woman every month." Noah picked up a pencil and began doodling on the pad.

"I figure you're doing the dating for both of us." Peter infused lightness into his voice because he didn't like the image of himself in a few years, alone, empty, but he didn't see any other alternative. "Now let's—"

The doorbell ringing cut into his words. Peter made his way to the front of his house and swung the door open. Laura and three of her children stood on the porch. The twins were punching each other in the arm, and Alexa smiled from ear to ear.

"Sorry we're late. When I walked out of the house

to come over here, I noticed I had a flat. Sean had to change it for me."

Laura's fresh, clean appearance appealed to Peter, but for some reason it also reminded him of Diana, which immediately brought up his guard. "I thought he was at school."

"No, he got through early." Laura shoved her car keys into her front pocket.

"Is he with you then?" While he pushed the screen door open, Peter peered behind the four on the porch.

"Nope. He'd rather stay home and do nothin'," one of the twins said as he entered the house.

Peter mouthed the word, "Who?" to Laura because he couldn't tell the boys apart yet.

A grin dimpled her cheek. "Matthew, hold up. Wait for us."

The seven-year-old stopped in the living room entrance with Joshua trailing behind. Blue T-shirt on Matthew. White on Joshua. Got it. Peter shut the door. "Jacob and Noah are in the dining room. Why don't you all go on back?"

Joshua scrunched up his forehead. "Who's Jacob and Noah?"

"Two friends."

"Our age?" Hope laced Matthew's question.

"Sorry, my age."

"Oh." Matthew's eager expression fell.

"But I've got some of the animals out back for you all to play with. They like it when I have visitors."

Joshua cocked his head to the side. "You don't get to play with them?"

Peter tousled his hair. "Not nearly as much as I would like. So will you help me out and play with them?"

"Sure." Matthew beamed, displaying a missing tooth.

"Shaggy is one of my original dogs, and he looks just like the one in the movie. He needs brushing. I left the brush on the patio. He got into some bushes in the field and I think he brought half of them back to the house. Can one of you take care of him?"

Joshua hopped from one foot to the other, his hand raised. "Me. Me."

Matthew punched his twin in the arm. "I love that movie. I want to do it."

"Why don't you two take turns? He's a big dog." Laura's two youngest were so full of life. *They brighten my home,* Peter thought.

"Will we get to ride again?" Alexa pointed to her sneakers and jeans. "I made sure I wore the right clothes for riding."

"Sure, if it's all right with your mom."

All three children faced Laura, the boys dancing about as though they couldn't contain themselves much longer.

"If we have time later. I still have to go to the grocery store on the way home from here."

Alexa took her mother's hand and tugged her toward the dining room. "Then you all better get busy."

The twins dashed ahead. Peter heard Noah and Jacob greet the kids then the back door banged close. When Peter stepped into the room, his friends were laughing.

"Who were those whirlwinds?" Jacob nodded toward Laura. "Nice to see you again."

"Those whirlwinds were my two sons, Joshua and Matthew." Laura placed a hand on her daughter's shoulder. "And this is Alexa, who needs to go keep an eye on them."

"Right, Mom." Alexa hurried after her brothers.

"It's a beautiful day. Let's move this planning meeting to the patio." Noah gathered up his pad and pencil and followed Alexa from the house with Jacob right behind him.

Peter put a hand on Laura's arm to stop her. "I haven't had a chance to ask how Lady's doing."

"Sean has decided he's going to start teaching her tricks today. The kids adore her. She sleeps with the twins one night and Sean the next. Poor Alexa doesn't have a chance with Lady because her brothers hog all her awake time."

"Maybe we should find a pet for Alexa." When he said *we*, it felt right and that bothered him until he reminded himself they were just friends and friends helped each other.

Peter opened his back door for Laura. "I know how much she liked Molly. She came with the ranch, and I would hate to take her away from here. I don't have any kittens right now, but I'm sure I'll get one before long."

She laughed. "Let's take it one pet at a time."

Out on the patio Peter slipped into the folding chair next to Laura. Noah and Jacob sat across the glass table of the patio set. Jacob watched the twins playing with the ferret. Noah scribbled something on the pad.

The sound of the boys' laughter floated in the air. Alexa's voice joined her brothers'. Peter leaned back, content to enjoy their merriment like music to his ears.

He'd wanted a whole houseful of children and that was never going to happen unless he married a woman with children. Was that why he was attracted to Laura against his better judgment? He knew he wouldn't be good husband material, and he couldn't let the fact that she had four children change his mind.

An hour later Jacob scooted his chair back from the glass table. "Okay. So we have a game plan. I like the idea of involving the church youth group with this project to get it started."

Noah rose. "I like the idea of using these abandoned animals to heal others." He looked at Laura. "Peter was always the idea man when we were growing up. He hasn't lost his touch."

Laura shifted her attention from one man to the other, her gaze finally lighting upon Peter. "Do you three go to the same church?"

"Jacob and I do. We haven't convinced Noah of the power of the Lord yet."

"I think this is my cue to leave." Noah grinned. "Bring your family by the restaurant one evening. I haven't found too many kids who don't like pizza."

Jacob pushed in his chair. "I'd better go, too. I have rounds at the hospital this afternoon."

The second Noah and Jacob left, Alexa ran up to Laura. "Can we go ride now?"

Laura scanned the yard. "Where's Matthew?"

Her daughter whirled around. "He was throwing the ball for Bosco."

Knowing her twins' gift for getting into trouble,

Laura shot to her feet, searching the area. A dog barking drew her down the steps and around the side of the house. She came to an abrupt halt when she found Matthew hanging off the side of Peter's two-story house, having climbed halfway up the stones.

Laura put her hands on her waist as Peter neared her. "Get down right now, young man. Whatever possessed you to climb up there?"

Matthew glanced over his shoulder while clinging to the brown stones. "The ball is up on the roof. I got carried away when I threw it. It's Bosco's favorite." His gaze skipped to the German shepherd sitting below him. "See? He's waiting for me to get it."

Getting carried away was the normal mode for her twins. "Come down before you break your neck." Visions of him falling flickered through her mind. He was her climber. As a toddler he had somehow found his way to the top of the refrigerator. Thankfully she'd gotten him down before he had fallen.

"All I have to do is go up here a little more, then along to the end and swing up—"

"Now!"

"Come on, Matthew. We're going riding. I'll get the ball later for Bosco."

"But, Mr. Stone…" The boy's gaze slid to his mother, and he started back down.

Peter moved closer at the same time she did. Matthew was two feet from the ground when Joshua raced around the side of the house with Alexa on his heels.

"Digger got away!"

The other twin's shouting caused Matthew to lose his

footing, and he fell back into Laura. His momentum threw her off balance, and she knocked against Peter like a set of dominos. They ended up on the ground, arms and legs tangling. Alexa giggled.

"Digger's gonna get away!" Joshua hopped from one foot to the other.

Blowing her son's hair from her face, Laura removed her elbow from Peter's ribs while Matthew extracted himself as though he were Houdini's protégé. He zipped around the side of the house after Joshua. Alexa and Bosco ran after the twins, leaving Laura alone to untangle herself from Peter.

"This reminds me of the time I played Twister." Peter slipped his arm from under her back and rolled to his feet. He offered her his hand.

She stared up at him. "We've got to stop meeting like this." She allowed him to help her up, feeling a few sore places where the hard ground had greeted her fall.

"Are you all right?"

"Are you?"

His eyes gleamed. "I asked first."

His nearness made her heart beat fast. She vaguely heard Bosco barking in the background. Her husband had been gone for almost a year, but their marriage had been in trouble for a long time before that. She hadn't felt this way in… She took a step back. There was no way she would get involved with a man again after her husband and his deceit. She couldn't go through that a second time. She didn't know if she could ever trust a man enough to put her heart in his hands again.

"We'd better check on the kids and Digger." She

started for the backyard, acutely aware of Peter's presence behind her.

"I know where he went. He goes under the house."

She halted, peering back at him. "Under the house?"

At the same time they both began running. When Laura arrived where Alexa was standing, the look on her daughter's face corroborated her suspicion that her twins had gone after Digger.

Alexa pointed at the opening. "They wouldn't listen to me. I told them not to go there."

Matthew and Joshua had selective hearing. They heard what they wanted to. Laura bent down and checked out the dark hole, visions of snakes, bugs and rats tumbling through her mind. Her fear escalated.

Peter moved between her and the opening. "I'll get them. I know where Digger likes to hide. I've had to do this several times."

"Ooh! Get it off me!"

Matthew's plea sent chills down Laura's spine. She started after Peter.

He held up his hand. "I'll take care of it. Both of us don't need to get dirty."

Laura nibbled on her thumbnail while she waited. Peter's voice when he reached her sons reassured her. She backed up as she saw them coming out. Both her sons were covered with dirt from head to toe.

Joshua's face was so brown that the whites of his eyes stood out like neon signs. "We got him! He's safe." His huge grin pronounced how proud he was of himself for "rescuing" the ferret from whatever evil vermin might dwell under the house.

Matthew crawled out and sprang to his feet, dancing about as he brushed at something in his hair. "I think there's a spider or something on me."

Laura placed her hands on his shoulders to keep him still long enough to check him while Alexa laughed. Laura wiped a cobweb and a twig from his hair. "You're okay. I don't see anything."

With Digger cradled in his arms, Peter emerged from the opening. "I don't understand how Digger got under here. This piece of wood usually keeps him out." He handed the ferret to Alexa while he secured the plywood over the hole.

Joshua's head dropped, his gaze glued to the ground.

Laura planted herself in front of him. "What happened?" When her son kept his head down, she continued, "Joshua, what did you do?"

Slowly he lifted his gaze to hers. "It was an accident. Really. All I did was put Digger down for just a second while I moved the wood a little to see what was behind it. Next thing I knew he had darted past me into the hole." He turned his attention to Peter. "I'm sorry, Mr. Stone. I didn't mean for him to get away like that. I won't let it happen again. Promise."

Peter gave Joshua the ferret. "Why don't you put him back in his cage so we can go riding?"

"You aren't mad?" Matthew asked, his eyes wide.

"It was an accident. I'm sure Joshua won't do it again now that he knows what can happen."

Laura remembered her husband in the last year before he'd died yelling at the twins for every little thing they'd done wrong. Their natural curiosity had been stifled. The sounds of her children's laughter had disappeared from their house. The memories produced a tight ache in her throat. At least that had returned to their home now.

"Coming?"

Peter's deep voice penetrated her journey into the past. She focused on his attractive face and couldn't help noticing the smile on it and a smudge of dirt on his forehead. She also noticed in that moment that she and Peter were the only two standing in front of the opening.

"Okay?"

She nodded, not sure her voice would work properly.

"You were miles away."

She swallowed several times. "Just thinking about something that happened a while back."

"Want to talk about it?"

The urge to tell him everything almost overrode the natural reserve she kept with most people. How could she explain what a failure she had been in her marriage? She hadn't seen the signs until it was too late, and she and her children had suffered.

"Where are the kids?" she asked, instead of giving in to the impulse to reveal her thoughts.

"They ran ahead to the barn."

She started forward. "Then we'd better hurry after them. I can just imagine what my sons will find to explore in there."

This was better. Telling Peter about her past would only leave her vulnerable. Instead she needed to toughen herself to stand alone.

Chapter Four

Cara, since I started working at the school three weeks ago, I know I haven't been faithful to e-mailing you like I should, but I'm taking a coffee break and using my time to e-mail you now. You're the only one I can really talk to, and I miss our early-morning coffee together. I'm sorry to hear about your husband's illness but hopefully it's nothing. Let me know the second you hear back about the tests he took.

Amazingly Sean has been a model child these past few weeks. Actually, the last couple of days he's been a real pleasure. A part of me is holding my breath waiting for the other shoe to drop. A part of me is celebrating I might have my child back. I know it's too early to be thinking that, but a mother can only hope.

Joshua and Matthew have added a few more gray hairs to my head. I caught them yesterday planning to jump from the back porch roof onto the mattress they had dragged out to the yard. They were practicing to be stuntmen. Where do they come up with these ideas? Then not long after that, Alexa comes in and wants to spend the night at Mindy Donaldson's Saturday then go to church with her on Sunday. I know what's coming next. She'll want to know why we aren't going to church anymore. How do I tell her my feelings on this? I know you don't understand why I'm angry with the Lord, but I really feel like He let me down. Break's over. I'll e-mail more later. Miss you guys. Love, Laura.

After hitting the send button, Laura glanced up from her computer screen and saw a teacher who'd lately become a friend. "Sadie, what brings you into the counseling office?"

"I need to check the credits on some of my students. Are you coming down to my room for our potluck lunch today?"

"Yep. I brought a tossed green salad."

"Great. That'll go well with what the others are bringing."

"See you then." Laura watched Sadie head back toward the registrar's office before concentrating on the report she was compiling now that her break was over.

The blaring sound of the fire alarm jolted her from her task. She looked up. No one was running for the doors. The few people in the outer office seemed to be waiting for the first person to leave. Laura dug into her bottom drawer and retrieved her purse. She would hate to replace the items in her bag if there really was a fire.

Sadie came from the back. "We'd better get outside."

"Ah, Mrs. Knight, it's just a false alarm," one of two student aides said, remaining in his chair.

Sadie winked at Laura, then turned a stern expression on the two teens. "False alarm or not, we need to leave. One day it could be the real thing. Besides, it's gorgeous outside."

Students and adults exited the counseling office. Laura took up the rear and started to shut the door when she heard the announcement. "False alarm. Please return to your classes."

Five minutes later, Laura sat again at her computer to finish the report. Her phone rang. When she picked it up and heard Peter's deep voice, dread filled her and her shoulders sagged.

"Are you sure it was Sean?" She desperately grasped onto the image of the picture-perfect child of the past few days, wanting him to remain.

"Afraid so, Laura. Sean pulled the fire alarm. We have him on tape."

Why did the students persist in doing something against the rules—and in front of the camera? Sean knew better. Embarrassment mixed with her disappointment. There was only one answer to that question, Laura decided as she stomped toward Peter's office for the second time in a month on account of her oldest child.

What did Sean think he was going to accomplish by pulling this stunt? Her chagrin quickly progressed to exasperation.

This time when she knocked on the principal's door, her hand didn't shake from being nervous but from her growing anger. What was she going to do about Sean?

Peter came out of his office and pulled her to the side. "Okay?"

"No. I don't know what to do next. Any suggestions?" The second she asked the question she wanted to snatch it back. Where was her resolve to become totally independent? The minute there was a problem she was asking him for advice. She needed to come up with a game plan on her own. But what?

"I have a strong suspicion he pulled the alarm to get out of coming to the ranch to work. He told me he was ready to serve Saturday school service tomorrow, and he'd make up his time for the FFA next weekend."

"Why'd he want to get out of working at the ranch?"

"Chad. He's the boy Sean got into a fight with and he's coming to work at the ranch."

"You bid on the boy Sean had a fight with?"

Peter's mouth quirked up in a grin. "I thought if the boys got together and worked as a team they may actually become friends."

She wanted to shout *Are you crazy?* But she kept her mouth shut.

"I know. That may not have been the best plan after all."

"You think? Sean holds grudges, at least lately. He didn't used to but so much about him has changed. You probably should take him up on his kind offer."

He shook his head. "No, he's got to learn he can't pull a prank and get out of something he doesn't want to do. He's dealing with a master in that area."

"So he's met his match?"

"Yep. You just wait and see."

She didn't want to depend on Peter with her son. She should be able to handle this on her own. And yet, what she was doing wasn't working.

"It'll turn out okay tomorrow. Besides, Brandon, the third boy, is one of our best student mediators. I've got it all figured out."

What had he been thinking when he bid on Sean *and* Chad at the FFA auction? Peter scratched his head and blew out a breath. What was happening in his barn would put the Cold War to shame. Constructing a pen together was supposed to have been a team-building project.

"Hold it still, will you!" Sean glared at Chad.

"If you'd work a little harder maybe we would actually get done this week." Chad glanced at his watch for the umpteenth time in the past hour.

And to make matters worse, his peacemaker, Brandon, couldn't come because he got sick. What was he thinking? *Lord, I need You. What do I do?*

"Here, let me, you guys." Peter stepped forward and helped hold the last board in place while Sean hammered several nails into the post to hold it.

Finished, all three of them stood back and inspected the animal pen. Two of the slats hung at an odd angle, but Peter wasn't going to say anything. At least it resembled what he had pictured in his mind.

When Laura's son's gaze lit upon one of the lopsided boards, Peter moved into Sean's line of vision, afraid that the Cold War would evolve into World War III. "Let's get Bessie and let her test out her new home. She's out in the back pasture."

Sean stomped off, mumbling under his breath.

"Mr. Stone, I don't get him. Nothing pleases Sean."

"Moving to a new town can be hard on some people."

"Why'd they come?"

"His father died. They have family here."

"Oh."

Chad had a big heart, and that was what Peter was counting on, why he had come up with this brilliant plan in the first place. Sean needed the right friends. At the moment he had no friends, but what he was really afraid of was that Sean would hook up with the wrong crowd when the boy decided to quit being a loner.

"Mr. Stone, come quick!"

Sean's shout prodded Peter into action. Chad hurried behind him. Out in the pasture Peter found Sean kneeling next to Bessie. The sheep had gone into labor. Worse, she was tangled in a thorny bush.

I should have pulled the wild roses up, Peter thought as he knelt next to the teen.

Sean turned his concerned gaze to Peter. "What do we do?"

For a few seconds Peter's mind went blank. The sheep's bleats filled the stillness and emphasized the seriousness of the situation, urging him into action. "We need to untangle her first, then we'll see if we can get her into the barn."

Five minutes later with all three of them working together, Bessie was free from the thorns, but Peter saw the head of a lamb.

"It's coming." Sean moved to Peter's side.

"There's a problem." Peter inspected the lamb's position, trying to remember what the vet had told him.

"Where's the front legs?" Chad situated himself on the other side of Peter.

"Yeah, we just read about that in class. A normal birth is front legs and head first." Sean moved his hand along the restless ewe's haunches.

"I don't think we have time to call the vet. We'll have to fix the problem and deliver the lamb here." Peter turned to Chad. "Go into the storeroom in the barn. On the left side on the third shelf I have what I need. A lubricant. A plastic sleeve and gloves. The disinfectant." While Chad leaped to his feet and raced for the barn, Peter shifted around to Sean. "I need a bucket of clean, warm water, soap and some towels. They're in the storeroom, too."

Before Peter had finished his sentence Sean shot up and followed Chad. Bessie tried to rise. Peter stilled her movements with his hands. He'd done some reading, too, and he knew that if the sheep got up and began running around with the lamb's head sticking out, there would be a bigger problem than going in to grab the feet.

Sweat broke out on Peter's forehead and rolled down into his eyes. "Bessie, it'll be all right. We're here to help."

Lord, I've delivered several foals before, but this is my first lamb. Surely it's similar. Please guide me.

"I've got it." Chad rushed up with his items cradled in his arms.

Peter threw a glance over his shoulder and saw Sean walking toward them at a slower pace to keep the water from sloshing out of the bucket. Laura's son placed it next to Peter then squatted, holding the soap and towels.

"Here goes. I'm going in to find the front legs. Your job is to keep Bessie as calm and still as possible. I don't want her getting up."

"Got it. We can do that." Sean's gaze captured Chad's across from him, and the other teen nodded, a grim expression on his face.

Peter washed his hands and arm thoroughly then did the same to the opening where the lamb's head was peeking out. After donning the sleeve and gloves and applying a lubricant, he took a deep breath and whispered, "Lord, be with me."

"Amen." Chad slid his gaze from Peter to Sean.

Several seconds later Laura's son replied the same.

Peter gently pushed the lamb's head back into the birth canal, then went in search of the front legs. "I feel something. A hoof. And another one."

Chad leaned close as if he could see what was going on inside. "Are the heels up or down?"

"Down. That's the front legs." Peter grabbed hold of both of them and began pulling them toward him.

"It's coming!"

The fervor in Sean's voice sent a responsive chord through Peter. He felt the teen's excitement as the lamb's shoulders appeared. When they had cleared, it shook its head. The membrane covering its nose ruptured. Soon it lay on the grass, sopping wet. Bessie struggled to her feet and began licking the lamb.

Peter watched for a few minutes while the sheep cleaned her baby, amazed at what had just happened, stunned that he had actually successfully delivered the lamb.

Sean jumped up, keeping a hand on the sheep's back, and shouted, "We did it!" He gave Chad a high five.

Peter examined Bessie. "I think another one is

coming. I see the legs. Sean, use the towels and dry this lamb off. We need to keep it warm. Mama is gonna be busy for a while."

"Yes, sir." Sean snatched up a towel and began working on the baby.

Laura parked near the barn and climbed from her car. As she walked toward the entrance, Peter came out, appearing as though he had fought a grizzly bear and lost. She hurried her steps. She should have stayed this morning instead of just dropping Sean off, especially with the sullen mood her son had been in. Had Sean and Chad gotten into another fight with Peter in the middle? "What happened?"

"One of my animals went into labor a little early. I was heading to the house to clean up. You aren't supposed to be here for another hour."

"I thought I would help you referee, but it looks like—" she peered around him into the barn "—you have everything under control."

Sean and Chad stood in the middle of a pen with an ewe and her two babies. Sean pointed at himself, blood from the birthing on his clothes, too, his hair plastered to his head with sweat. Then her son grinned from ear to ear at Chad, who said something to Sean. He laughed. A wonderful sound she hadn't heard much lately.

Laura turned back to Peter. "What have you done to my son? He's laughing."

He shrugged. "We just delivered two lambs a little while ago."

"That's all! Is this an everyday occurrence?"

Peter combed his fingers through his messy hair. "I'm hoping not. I'm glad Chad and Sean were here. Bessie had a few problems."

Her gaze traveled down his length. "A few?"

"Okay, we nearly lost both lambs. I might have if Sean hadn't found Bessie in time."

Again Laura looked at her son who was kneeling next to one of the babies. Awe graced his features as though he couldn't believe what he was seeing. For a minute, she couldn't believe her eyes, either. Her son happy, at peace.

"I'm going up to the house to get some sodas for them. Can you come with me and take the sodas back to the boys while I clean up? They don't seem to mind being dirty and smelly—" Peter wrinkled his nose "—but I do."

Chad left the pen and crossed to a faucet. After turning the water on, he hosed himself down, then passed it to Sean who had joined him.

"Nor do they particularly care how they clean up." Laura started toward Peter's house. "I almost didn't leave Sean this morning. I was sure you didn't know what you were doing when you insisted on both boys working together today."

"Why do you say that?"

She stopped halfway across the yard, shielding her eyes from the sun with her hand while staring into the laughter in his gaze. "It's not every day, thankfully, that a student pulls the fire alarm to get out of working at his principal's ranch for the FFA because he's sure he'll get Saturday school service instead."

Peter chuckled. "Don't tell Sean, but I did that once in middle school, and your son will get Saturday school service. He'll just have to do it the next two weekends."

She began walking again. "You know why he did it. So you see why I was worried. I would have been here even earlier, but I had to take Alexa to Mindy's to spend the night and the twins to soccer practice."

At the back door Peter opened it for her and waited until she entered his house first. "When do you have to pick Joshua and Matthew up from practice?"

"That's the beauty. I don't. Sadie Knight is bringing them home after they go out to Fast Eddie's for hamburgers."

"So you had a little time to kill and decided to come rescue me. Well, ma'am, I'm mighty appreciative, but I don't need saving." He opened the refrigerator and removed a six-pack of sodas.

"But you do need a shower." She plucked the drinks from his hand and headed for the door, his laughter following her outside.

The memory of that sound stayed with her all the way back to the barn. Nearing the entrance another noise replaced it in her mind, and she quickened her pace.

"That's my lamb. Yours is that one over there."

Sean's shouts echoed through the cavernous barn, making her clutch the cold sodas against her front so she wouldn't drop them as she jogged inside to find her son and Chad squaring off in the middle of the pen where only moments before there had been a tranquil bonding scene. What had happened?

"Sean?" Laura rushed toward the two teens.

He swung around, his arms rigid at his sides, his chest rising and falling rapidly as he sucked air into his lungs. "Mr. Stone said I could look after a lamb and I want to take care of that one." He gestured to the bigger of the two, sucking milk from its mother.

Laura opened her mouth to say something but couldn't think of anything to say so she snapped it closed, hoping that Peter took quick showers. "Sodas, anyone?" Thankfully they were all the same. No fight there.

Chad left the pen and approached her. "Thanks, Mrs. Williams." He took one, popped it open and nearly drained it in a couple of gulps. Then he grabbed another one.

Sean charged over and snatched two sodas, a mutinous expression on his face. Everything was a big deal to her son lately, even drinking a Dr Pepper was becoming a competition. He started back toward the pen when Chad did. They bumped shoulders as they both tried to go through the opening at the same time. Whirling around, they glared at each other.

Laura placed the two cans she held on the ground, ready to throw herself in between the two teens if they began fighting. She remembered a teacher at school advising her last week never to break up a fight in the hall by stepping into the middle of it. But what else could she do? Watch her son get beaten up? Chad was several inches taller, not to mention forty pounds heavier than Sean. And those forty pounds had to be all muscle. Chad was a tackle on the football team. What was Sean thinking?

Her son inched closer to the other teen, a soft drink in each hand. Chad leaned in, meeting him glare for glare. Laura frantically scanned the barn for something to stop a fight before it started. She saw the hose. She rushed to it and turned the faucet on.

Just as Sean threw down both sodas, she whipped the arc of water in their direction. Dousing the two teens sent them flying backward and toward her. Both pairs of eyes grew round. Soaking wet, her son shoved hair out of his face while Chad started laughing. For a few seconds Sean remained stunned, then suddenly he laughed, too.

Peter came up behind her and took the hose from her hands. "Remind me never to antagonize you. You're lethal with a hose."

She glanced down at her "weapon," now turned off and limp in Peter's grasp. "I can't believe it worked."

"It's called shock therapy," Peter whispered then strode forward. "What's the problem?"

Laura tensed, waiting for the two teens to remember why they'd almost gotten into a fight a few minutes before.

"Nothing Sean and I can't handle, Mr. Stone."

"Yeah, just a friendly disagreement. You can have that one." Sean waved his hand toward the lamb they had been arguing over. "I kinda like runts."

Laura stuck her finger in her ear and wiggled it. Had she heard right? Maybe her son had finally gotten a good look at Chad and how big the teen was.

"I appreciate you all keeping an eye on them. They need to stay warm and nurse. I'm gonna feed the other animals. You two play nice while Laura and I are gone." Peter peered at her. "Do you mind helping?"

"No, what do you want me to do?"

He went into a supply room near the front of the barn and came out with four bags a few minutes later. "This is ferret, cat, rabbit and dog food." He held up each one, then passed the cat and rabbit food to her. "I feed the cats on the back patio. You know where the rabbit cages are. I'll take care of the dogs and ferret."

"Any new animals since the last time I was here?"

"Other than one kitten and the ewe that just gave birth to two lambs, no."

"A sheep and a kitten in a few weeks. Have you given any away?"

"Lady was the last one." He tossed her a cocky grin. "We've got to have animals if we are going to use them with at-risk children."

Laura exited the barn with Peter, glancing over her shoulder at her son who stared down at his lamb as if it were the most fascinating creature he had ever seen. "It seems to be working." A couple of steps toward the backyard and she asked, "Did Sean do everything you wanted him to do today?"

"Other than we didn't get a chance to fix the fence in the back pasture, yes he did. Bessie interrupted the work flow."

"How are the plans coming for the animal center?"

"Okay, but something just doesn't seem right. I'm missing something."

She paused and tilted her head. "What?"

"As soon as I figure it out, I'll let you know. God's

got something special planned, but He isn't ready to reveal it to me yet."

"He might never reveal it."

For a fleeting moment surprise flickered into his expression, but it quickly left. "Why do you say that?"

"How do you know what God really wants? It's not like He shouts it for the whole world to hear."

"Sometimes I think he does. Occasionally I'm not listening, and He smacks me upside my head to get my attention."

Laura opened the first rabbit cage and scooped the food pellets into the bowl. "Have you ever prayed and not been answered?"

"I've gotten an answer, but it just might not be the one I want to hear. God works in His time, not ours."

Frustration churned her stomach as she closed the rabbit cage. "What happens when He abandons you?"

"He doesn't."

She rounded on him, clutching the two bags against her chest. "How do you know that?" After the past year she felt abandoned.

His intense gaze drilled into her. He splayed his hand over his heart. "I know in here. There was a time I didn't listen to Him, and I nearly ended up in jail and on a path of self-destruction that could have led to prison. He took me by the shoulders and shook some sense into me."

"He did?" The mockery leaked through her words.

"Well, not Him actually but his instrument, Paul Henderson."

"Your foster father?"

"Yes, that man and his wife saved me and at the time I didn't even know I wanted to be saved. He wouldn't let me pull any of my usual tricks when I went to a new foster home."

She approached the next rabbit cage and put the food inside. "Like what?"

"I would sneak out at night. Guess who was waiting for me each time I tried? But Paul never got angry at me. He would just talk to me. At first I wouldn't say anything, but before long I began pouring out my feelings, my anger to him. That was the best therapy. Keeping all that anger inside eats away at a person."

"Why were you so angry?" She remembered her e-mails to Cara and the talks they used to have in St. Louis when they lived next door to each other. She missed that and wished she had someone closer to confide in, but it wasn't easy for her to tell anyone her problems. If Cara hadn't lived so close and been aware of what went on in her house, she would never had opened up to her in the first place.

Peter moved to the large ferret cage under the awning on the patio. Digger inspected what he put into his bowl, trying to eat the food before Peter finished. "My father left my mom when I was born so I never knew him, but she was always wonderful with me. We didn't have much. Some days I didn't get enough to eat. My mom worked two jobs to put a roof over our heads and food on the table. I think it wore her out. She died when I was ten, and I went into the foster care system because I had no relatives the state could find to take me in."

"Did you move around a lot?"

"Not at first, but as I got older and angrier, I started doing things to get me kicked out of a house. From twelve to fifteen I was in eight different homes." He started to bend over to pour the dry food into one of the large dog bowls, stopped and straightened, looking into her eyes with all the pain from his past blazing in their depths. "There aren't enough good foster homes around. Paul and Alice Henderson's was my last chance."

"Have you ever thought about taking a child in?"

Peter filled the metal container with a day's worth of dog food for Bosco and Shaggy. "Yes. I've even thought about adoption." He walked to the hose and picked it up.

"What's stopping you?"

His eyes widened as though her question had taken him by surprise. "You know, nothing really. But…" His voice faded into the silence.

Transfixed by the thoughtful look that took over Peter's expression, she waited for him to finish what he was about to say. His silence lengthened. A bird chirped in a nearby tree. Bosco came bounding around the side of the house and up to his bowl, eating with a slurping sound. Molly ambled over to Laura and meowed, peering up at the food container as if she could read the word cat on it. Another loud meow jarred Laura into action, and she quickly fed Molly.

When she turned back to Peter, a huge grin was plastered on his face. She arched an eyebrow.

"I've got it! I don't want to take care of just one child when there are so many who need it. Paul and Alice taught me that. They didn't adopt the kids who came through their house because they wanted to be available for whomever needed a home. They wanted to touch as many children as possible and they did. What if I use the land I have to open a home for foster children?"

"Build another house?"

He began to pace. "Yes. I'd have to raise money, probably start some kind of foundation."

Laura exhaled a deep breath. "Wow. That's ambitious."

"Think what we could do with the animals and the kids."

When she heard him say *we,* she should have panicked. But for some reason it felt right to be included in his plans. The thought of helping others appealed to her, too.

"Are you willing to meet again with Noah and Jacob? I'd like to brainstorm this idea and see what needs to be done first."

His excitement charged the air, sparking her own desire to help. She knew the need was there, and she was tired of standing on the sidelines. Maybe that was what she needed, to get involved with a worthy cause. For too long she had been focused on her own problems. "Yes, I can. I don't know how much I can contribute. I have done some fund-raising for my kids' school while in St. Louis. I was on the board of its foundation that raised money for teacher projects."

"That's great!" Peter quickly turned on the faucet and began filling the water bowls for the various pets. "Maybe we can involve some kids in this, too."

"It would be good for Sean, but getting him to think that may be a problem."

After quickly finishing up feeding the rest of the animals, Peter headed toward the barn. "Leave that to me."

How easy would it be to leave everything to Peter? I can't do that. He has enough on his plate. I need to take care of my family. "I appreciate your offer, but Sean's my problem."

A few feet from the entrance into the barn Peter came to a stop and faced her. "Friends help friends."

Is that what they were, friends? She hadn't had a male friend in years, since before she was married. It seemed so strange. "Speaking of friends. This might be right up Sadie's alley. I also met Mindy Donaldson's mom, Tory. Do you know she uses horses for therapy with children with special needs?"

"I've heard of her."

"She might want to help, too."

Peter snapped his fingers. "I've got an idea. Why don't I throw a party to recruit people to help? I could feed them then ask them if they would like to be a part of this project."

"I can help you with the party. A barbecue would be nice."

"How about a hayride to the stream at the back edge of my ranch where we would have a barbecue set up?"

"What if it rains?"

"It hasn't in over a month but you're right. The second we plan something outdoors without a backup plan, it would rain. We could have the party in the barn if it does."

"Speaking of no rain, what if the governor bans outdoor grilling like he's thinking of doing?"

Peter raised both eyebrows. "You are thorough. I hadn't thought about that. Then we'll just have a picnic, no grilling involved. How's two weeks from today sound to you?"

"Great!"

"What's great, Mom?" Sean sauntered up to them.

"We were planning a party."

Her son scowled. "Why?"

"Peter wants to start a foundation to provide a foster home here on his ranch."

"That sounds neat, Mr. Stone." Chad joined them. "I know a guy at school that lives in one, but he isn't too happy right now."

Peter's gaze fastened onto Chad. "Who?"

"Rob Somers."

"The pitcher for the baseball team?" Sean's scowl dissolved into a puzzled expression. "He's so popular."

Chad glanced toward her son. "I shouldn't have said anything," he mumbled, swinging his attention to Mr. Stone. "Forget what I said. I'd better get back inside. My lamb has been nursing a lot."

"Mine isn't. I came out here to tell you that."

"I'll be in there in a minute. The vet warned me this might happen. I'll have to rig something up to make sure it gets what it needs."

As the boys left, Sean asked Chad where Rob lived. Chad didn't answer him right away, and Laura prepared herself for her son to lash out at Chad for ignoring his question. But Sean didn't. He waited patiently until the other teen answered him with the address.

"Rob's pretty open about his situation, but I try not

to say too much about it with him." Chad opened the gate to the pen.

Sean stepped inside first. "Why not?"

"Just because."

As Laura leaned against the wooden slats, Sean knelt next to his lamb, stroking it. "I'd never thought that of Rob. He's always so upbeat at school. I have him in one of my classes."

"That's Rob. He doesn't let things get him down." Chad led the sheep over to Sean's lamb and helped her son try to coax the small lamb to nurse.

The pensive expression on her son's face piqued Laura's curiosity. Was Sean comparing his situation to Rob's? Her son thought his life was bad right now. Getting him involved with kids with even greater needs might be what would help him come to terms with his father's death. And she had Peter to thank for that.

Chapter Five

Laura glanced up from her computer while composing an e-mail to Cara about the next day's barbecue and the prediction of rain in the forecast. She stared at the beige coverlet on her bed. It wouldn't hurt to pray. Maybe it would do some good.

She bowed her head. "Lord, please keep the rain away until tomorrow night. And while I'm talking to You, please have people get excited about Peter's project. It means so much to him."

In her heart she sensed the party would be a success. For a long moment she let a tranquil feeling encase her before she focused again on her e-mail to her friend.

The best part about the party is Sean is excited and helping with the plans. Yesterday he asked Peter if he could drive the wagon and Peter said yes. My son floated around the rest of the day. I've had to take Sean out to the ranch every day after work to check on "his lamb." Thankfully it is thriving. I don't know what I would have done if Peter hadn't managed to help it eat. I think at that moment Sean's opinion of Peter began to change, especially when he let my son stay with him in the barn all night to make sure the lamb lived.

I'd better go. It's late and tomorrow will be a long day. I hope this specialist can figure out what's wrong with your husband. You would think after all the tests Mason has gone through they would have an idea what's going on. You and your family are in my thoughts as always. Love, Laura.

She stared at the computer screen, went back in and changed the wording to "in my prayers," instead of "in my thoughts," then sent the e-mail.

Lord, I'm back with another request. Please help the doctors come up with what's going on with Mason. He's in so much pain. If You don't want to do it for me, please do it for Cara.

As Sean drove the wagon toward the stream, he sat tall and straight on the bench. Alexa and her friend Mindy were next to him. Content, Laura sighed, scanning the faces of the others in the back on top of the mound of loose hay. When a piece stuck her in her left shoulder, she shifted closer to Peter to try and get more comfortable. He looked at her, his features shadowed by his Stetson. But she saw the smile that reached deep into his eyes, riveted totally on her. His regard made her feel special as if he were only interested in her. That was Peter's way—to concentrate on the person he was talking to as though there was no one else in the world. She shouldn't read more into it, or should she? No wonder people responded to him.

The past few weeks of working on the party had thrown them together a lot. She found herself telling him about her life in St. Louis. She'd even come close to sharing the disastrous past year with him, dealing with the growing verbal abuse—the time Stephen went too far. No! Getting that close would throw their relationship to a whole new level she wasn't ready for.

"I'm glad we didn't have to go to Plan B." Peter peered up at the cloudless sky. "Although I feel guilty for not wanting it to rain."

Laura chuckled. "Me, too." She tossed back her head and let the warm rays of the sun bathe her face. "I even e-mailed my friend in St. Louis about not wanting it to rain. You think that's what did it?"

He shrugged. "Do you miss not living in St. Louis?"

"I miss Cara. She was my next-door neighbor and we're close. It's tough not being around while her husband is so sick. The doctors can't figure out what's wrong, but he's been in and out of the hospital over the past few weeks in a great deal of pain. We keep in touch by e-mail and phone. Not the same thing, though."

"No. Face-to-face is so much better. Even teens are really getting into communicating via blogging and text messaging. The upside is that it may help their writing skills some."

"But not their verbal skills?"

"Right. And some of those Internet sites where teens post about their day, their thoughts, are prime places for people who prey on kids."

Laura leaned close, not wanting Sean to hear. "So far I haven't found anything that Sean has posted, but I'm sure going to keep an eye on him and Alexa."

"I wish more parents would do that. Did you read in the paper where they caught that thirty-year-old man stalking that teenage girl? He found her through her blog. She gave away too much personal information. It wasn't hard for him to track her down."

She pulled back. The scent of hay, earth and Peter overwhelmed her, making her acutely aware of the man beside her. "I know. I've had a chat with all my kids. Thankfully Joshua and Matthew are too busy trying to find a way to build the fastest go-cart to be interested in the Internet. But I find Alexa is using it more and more."

"Parents have so much to worry about today."

"We're here." Sean pulled on the reins to stop the horses.

Chairs and tables had been set up earlier that morning under the large maple and oak trees that offered some shade. The stream ran through the glade ten feet away from their party site, the sound of water flowing over rocks soothing. Several grills were off to the side with large ice chests nearby, packed with chicken and beef kabobs for the adults and hamburgers for the kids.

Perfect, Laura thought as she relished the seventy-degree temperature with a light breeze from the south.

Sean twisted around on the bench. "I'll go back and get the others."

The twins, along with Sadie's son, hopped down first and charged toward the creek. Alexa and Mindy followed.

"Want me to go with you?" Andrew Knight, Sadie's husband, helped a pregnant Sadie down.

"Nope, I've got it."

Laura looked at Peter, wondering if he would overrule her son and insist an adult go with him. Peter remained quiet as he climbed down then offered his hand up to her. She mouthed, "You okay with that?"

He nodded.

When she grasped him to steady herself, a jolt streaked up her arm as though she had handled a live wire. Her heart beat a little faster. Lately when she touched him, her body reacted. She couldn't seem to control it. She clambered over the side and quickly put some space between them before she began to hyperventilate in his presence—and everyone else's.

"I asked Aunt Sarah if she wanted to join us. She laughed and told me her days of riding in the back of a wagon were definitely over. She values a padded seat."

"My foster mom Alice said about the same thing, although I'm to give her a report on what we decide to do."

Laura watched the kids fan out to explore the area. Her twins and Sadie's son had already found a tree to climb. "The higher they can go the better they like it."

"No more attempts to jump from the roof?" Peter lifted the lid on one ice chest and withdrew several sodas.

"No, but you know that big elm tree in Aunt Sarah's backyard? They asked her if they could build a fort in it and she said yes."

Peter handed her a can. "What's wrong with that?"

"Hello. Broken body parts."

He chuckled. "I don't think you can stop them." He gestured toward the sweet gum a few feet from the creek, the three boys several branches up into it.

"I know," she said with a sigh.

In the distance she saw the wagon returning with the rest of the party. Jacob Hartman sat next to Sean up front. Bosco hung over the side with Noah's hand on the dog as if that would stop him from jumping to the ground. Bosco and her twins were a lot alike. Forces to be reckoned with.

"Are we eating first or discussing your plans?" Sadie came up to them with her husband.

"Leave it to my wife to be the first one to ask about the food." Andrew cradled his arm around Sadie.

She smiled up into his face. "I'm eating for two."

"I've heard that a few times these past few months."

Laura looked at the pair, their gazes trained on each other, and for a fleeting moment missed that closeness with a man. Then she remembered her husband's secretive life and didn't think she could ever let down her guard enough to fall in love again.

"Look on the bright side. You only have four more months to listen to that." Out of the corner of her eye Laura noticed Sean bringing the wagon to a stop.

Sadie groaned. "Don't remind me how long I have. Four long months, mostly during the heat of an Oklahoma summer. The middle of August can't get here fast enough."

"I'm making an executive decision. Let's eat first, then talk." Peter turned to greet the others who arrived.

Noah assisted his date down from the wagon while Sean, Jacob and Bosco jumped down. Slade Donaldson started to offer his hand up to his wife, but Tory leaped to the ground before his arm was halfway up. She walked around to the two horses, patted them, then helped Sean unhook the harness.

"I'm glad you could make it," Peter said as Noah and his date approached, a beautiful, slender woman in her late twenties with long blond hair. "Is everything okay?"

"Sure. I just had to swing by the restaurant before picking up Anne." Noah brought his date forward. "This is Anne Laskey. When she heard about what we were planning to do, she wanted in."

Anne shook everyone's hands in the circle. "My daddy is always looking for a good cause to support."

Even Laura, a new resident of Cimarron City, knew who Anne's daddy was. He was the president of the largest bank and in the news quite a bit. Very involved in the town. Maybe Peter's idea had a good chance of working. She hoped so because the more she thought about what Peter wanted to accomplish the more she wanted to be part of it.

When Laura pulled out a paper and pen, Peter smiled. "You are efficient. I'd heard rumors at school that you were."

"You have?" She set the pad in her lap.

"Oh, yes. All the counselors rave about how you run the office."

"I figure someone has to write down what we talk about today."

"Like I said, efficient. What are you going to do this summer?" Since Laura's job was only for ten months, she'd be off for all of June and July. Although they didn't see each other a lot during the school day, he enjoyed knowing she was in the building.

"I have four kids to keep me busy. Money will be tight, but I can use the time to help Aunt Sarah fix the duplexes up. She's been wanting to do it, but then she got sick."

"If this project gets going, I could use your help. Would you like to be part of it?"

"Yes. If you hadn't asked for my help, I was going to volunteer it."

The pen rolled off and fell to the ground. Peter bent to retrieve it at the same time Laura did. They bumped shoulders and barely missed hitting their heads. She pulled away while his fingers clasped around the ballpoint. When he gave it to her, the flushed tint to her cheeks reflected his own reaction. He felt as though he had never dated before and was just learning the rules and making a fumbling mess of it. And when he really thought about it, he couldn't believe he felt that way because this was not even a date! Laura would be the first to make that clear. He'd considered himself gun-shy when it came to having a relationship with someone again, but Laura had him beat by a mile.

"Thanks," she murmured and held on to the pen.

Before beginning the discussion, Peter waited until the other adults sat down in the folding chairs he'd put in a circle. Off to the side Joshua, Matthew and Sadie's son began scaling another tree while Alexa and Mindy walked along the creek. Sean joined them in the circle. The sounds of nature serenaded the group as they settled in.

"Thank you all for coming today. I want to make a difference to some needy kids and I'd like to talk about building a foster home on my ranch. I have plenty of room. Does anyone have any suggestions on how to begin?" Peter scanned his friends' faces.

"That's ambitious. I'm not sure how to go about doing it."

Tory's words hung in the air for a few seconds before Noah said, "However you do it, it will require money, a lot of it."

Other than Noah, Peter didn't know very many wealthy people. "So do we start a nonprofit organization then begin raising that money?"

Anne lifted her hand as though she were in class and wanted to be called on. "I know Daddy's bank deals with nonprofit groups. I can ask him to help."

"That's great." Peter shifted in his chair, not sure how to respond to Noah's latest, gorgeous date, much like all the rest he saw for a short time. His friend made it a point to go out with women who would never really interest him in the long run. He was determined to remain single, and after Peter's disastrous marriage, he wondered if maybe Noah was right. However, he'd taken the opposite approach and just didn't date much at all. "Let's say we get the organization set up. What kind of fund-raiser can we have to bring in funds?"

Laura tapped the pen against the pad. "Why not a

dinner auction? I organized one for the school foundation in St. Louis. We made nearly fifty thousand."

Jacob whistled. "That's a good start. Although the cost of building one house will be at least four times that amount. How's a dinner auction work?"

"We get people and businesses to contribute, then for the smaller items we have a silent auction and for the bigger ones we have a live auction where an auctioneer presents each item and the audience bids on it. It can get very competitive and bring in more money." Laura wrote on her paper. "Sort of like Noah and Peter at the FFA auction last month."

"We're always competitive, since high school." Noah chuckled. "This fund-raiser can be a great promotion for a business, too."

"With you being a member of the Chamber of Commerce, Noah, I'm going to count on you to help us in that area." *If this is God's will then He will make it happen,* Peter thought when he contemplated everything that would have to be done before the foundation could be poured for the house.

Noah nodded. "That I can do and more."

"You'll need to get the media involved. You'll need a lot of publicity to get people to contribute to the auction as well as come." Sadie lumbered to her feet and stretched.

"Anyone have connections with the television station, newspaper, radio?" Excitement began to bubble in the pit of Peter's stomach. This could work.

"I do."

Again Noah spoke up and Peter wasn't surprised. His

friend knew how to network, which would come in handy. "I run ads on both the radio and television stations. And the editor in chief of the newspaper is a friend."

Sean cocked his head to the side, his forehead creased. "Why aren't there enough foster homes for kids?"

Peter clasped the arms of his folding chair. "That's a good question. In a perfect world there would be plenty of places for children who need a good home."

Sean scowled. "But this isn't a perfect world." Anger touched his voice.

"No, it isn't. Noah, Jacob and I grew up in foster care. We know firsthand some of its problems. A lot of the people who take in children mean well, but there are some who don't. There are some who think it's a business and treat the kids as a commodity. I want a place that is safe and where the children come first while they wait to be adopted or go back home."

Sean stared at him for a moment, then blinked and averted his gaze, but not before Peter had seen his earlier anger dissolving and changing. Hope flared in him. The boy was floundering and wrestling with something he wasn't ready to share with others. He knew the signs because he had been there. It had taken Paul to open the dam on Peter's emotions. Could he do the same for Sean?

Lord, show me the way.

When Peter swung his attention to Laura, he found her watching him with almost the same expression as her son. What was she grappling with? He wanted to be there for her, too, but at the same time worry nibbled at his thoughts. Getting involved with Laura might involve his heart.

Jacob cleared his throat.

Everyone was staring at him. Peter swallowed several times, desperately seeking a way to take the focus off him. "So when do we want to have this auction?" With restless energy surging through him, Peter rose. He wanted to go back to his house and start right away.

"Let's shoot for the weekend after Labor Day."

Peter peered at Laura. "Why then? Why not in June, or July, or for that matter, August even?"

Laura laughed. "Patience. If you want it done well, we'll need time to plan and organize it. Besides, people are on vacation during the summer. When school starts next year, everyone will be around and hopefully ready to donate their hard-earned money to a worthy cause."

Peter moved behind his folding chair and gripped its back. "Okay, that makes sense. Planning the auction won't be the only thing we'll be doing between now and September. We'll need to get the nonprofit organization up and running."

Noah leaned forward, planting his elbows on his thighs. "There's no reason you can't start soliciting donations before the auction. I can talk to Bill at the newspaper about a series of articles concerning the foster care system in Cimarron City to let the townspeople know about the need for more places to house the children."

"Then the paper can do an article about the Henderson Foundation." Peter watched Noah and Jacob's faces brighten with smiles. "I want to name the organization after Paul and Alice."

Jacob cheered. "You'll get no argument from—"

"Mrs. Williams!" Mindy's shout cut Jacob off and brought Laura to her feet, the pad and pen falling to the ground. "Alexa has been bitten by a snake." Mindy appeared at the edge of the circle of chairs, her face pale, her eyes huge.

Jacob leaped up. "Where is she?"

As Peter asked everyone to stay back, Laura rushed after Mindy with Jacob and Peter right behind her. Twenty yards downstream near some tall grass Alexa sat, tears coursing down her cheeks. Her daughter held a hand over a place below her right knee at the side of her calf. The ashen cast to her features quickened Laura's pace. Her daughter's sobs knifed into her.

Laura arrived and positioned herself next to Alexa, then inspected the area, wishing she could get hold of the snake who had hurt her daughter. "Honey, are you all right? Let us see the bite."

Jacob and Peter knelt near Alexa's legs while Laura grasped her daughter's upper arms and embraced her. Alexa removed her hand from the bite. Two fang marks stood out—red, nasty looking, blood oozing from the site.

"Alexa, do you know what kind of snake it was?" Jacob probed the skin surrounding the wound.

"I thought I heard a rattle right before it struck Alexa." Mindy drew in several quick gulps of air.

"I think—" Alexa inhaled a shuddering breath "—it was a rattlesnake. I saw one at the zoo once."

The pain in her daughter's voice tore at Laura's composure. She squeezed her eyes closed for a few seconds, fear immobilizing her.

Jacob turned to Peter. "Get the horses hooked up. We need to get her to the hospital. I'll need something to hold her leg still. A board. Anything you can find. Also a way to tie her leg to it."

Peter shot to his feet. "Got it. Be right back." He threw Laura a gaze loaded with concern then whirled around and ran toward the picnic area.

She heard him tell someone to get the horses and wagon ready. "What can I do?" Helplessness swamped her while Jacob pulled out a folded handkerchief from his pocket and began tying it around her daughter's leg right above the bite.

While he inserted a finger between the cotton material and Alexa's leg, he glanced up at her. "We need to keep Alexa's bite lower than her heart."

She pointed at the bandage. "Don't you need to make that tighter like a tourniquet?"

"No. I don't want to stop the blood flow, just slow it down some." Jacob gave her and Alexa a reassuring smile. "You're going to be all right. When we get to the hospital, we'll get you an antivenin and you'll be as good as new in a few days."

The tears continued to streak her daughter's face. "It hurts."

Laura's stomach knotted, and she tried to keep the fear out of her voice. "I know, baby." She wound her arms around her daughter and held her back against her.

"Will this do?" Peter presented Jacob with the top of a cooler and several belts.

"Yes." Jacob gently lifted Alexa's leg onto the plastic board and began fastening the belts around her and the cooler top, tight enough to keep her leg immobilized but not too tight to cut off her blood flow.

Slade Donaldson approached. "We've got the wagon ready."

Jacob stood. "Good. Let's carry her to it. Make sure to keep her leg down."

While the three men carried Alexa toward the wagon, Laura grasped her daughter's hand. There was a cold clammy feel to her skin. Sweat poured off Alexa, and her breathing was now shallow. The knot in Laura's stomach tightened into a huge stone.

Lord, please don't let anything happen to Alexa. If You are mad at me, then take it out on me, not her. Please.

She'd prayed to God and He had listened this time. The way Alexa responded to the treatment at the hospital led the doctor to feel that not much venom had gotten into her system. Laura plopped down at her kitchen table, cradling the mug of herbal tea between her cold hands.

The scrape of the chair as Peter pulled it out and sat reverberated through the room. His gaze captured hers. A smile entered his eyes. "Are you all right?"

"No—yes. As long as Alexa is fine, I'm fine."

"It was sure nice of everyone to clean up when we left for the hospital and to tell me they'd still be willing to help get my dream going."

She couldn't take her attention from his endearing

features. He had been her rock today. While Jacob had seen to Alexa, Peter had been by her side, making sure she was okay. When she was married to Stephen she'd never had that. Her deceased husband had often been unavailable when an emergency had occurred. She could remember Joshua falling off his bike and busting open his head. He'd needed seven stitches. But that wasn't what had frightened her so much. It was the amount of blood. When she had come home after spending hours at the hospital, she'd glanced down and finally noticed her shirt and pants were covered and caked in her son's blood. And Stephen still hadn't arrived home. Now she knew where he'd been. Gambling their life savings away.

"Your daughter was great." Peter's voice interrupted her unpleasant memories.

"Yes, she's a good girl." Laura took a sip of her drink, its warmth sliding down her dry throat.

"I promised her I would let her ride next weekend. That is if she's up to it and you say it's okay." One corner of his mouth quirked upward. "It got a smile out of her."

"No doubt. She loves going to Mindy's and riding. I have a hard time saying no to her. She doesn't ask for much." With Mindy and Peter at least she could give one of her children their dream. Being a good parent wasn't easy. Being a good single parent was even harder. "Alexa wants me to take her to church tomorrow."

"That's great!"

Laura stared down at her tea. "If I do, I would feel like a hypocrite. I don't know how I feel about the Lord.

I'm so confused. I prayed today to Him to take care of Alexa and He did. But I prayed a lot this last year for Him to help us and He didn't. We still lost our home, had to move in with Aunt Sarah, leave all our friends in St. Louis." The second she told Peter that she wanted to take it back. The door on her past had cracked open and she'd given him a glimpse into it. Instead of putting it behind her, she kept returning to it. Would the memories ever go away?

"Have you ever thought that maybe that's what He wanted for you and your family? That He has a plan in all this?"

Exhaustion clung to her. Coldness seeped deep into her bones. Laura hovered over the tea, seeking the warmth drifting upward. "I don't know. I'm just so afraid I'm gonna lose my son. The only time I see him happy is when he's with the animals at your place or playing with Lady."

Peter reached across the table and took her hands within his. "Bring the whole family to church tomorrow, not just Alexa. We have a wonderful youth program. I'm going to use them to help work with the animals and at-risk children. Maybe Sean will become involved."

"I'm not sure I can get him to come. He's awfully angry with God." *Like his mother. Is he mirroring my feelings? Or, is it something more?*

"Give him the opportunity. He may surprise you. And you aren't being a hypocrite. It's okay to ask questions, to have doubts. We all have at one time or another. If you want I can come by and pick you all up. I can introduce you around. I suspect I know everyone who attends."

How did he manage to get her to say so much to him? Afraid of what was happening to her, she pulled her hands back and placed them in her lap. "No, if I decide to go, I can take them. Besides, after today Alexa may not feel like going. She never goes to bed this early. I know she has a high threshold for pain, but she isn't feeling well. Thankfully the doctor said she would be all right coming home as long as she took it easy because she didn't want to stay there." She was offering every excuse she could come up with, not because of the idea of going to church, but because she didn't want Peter to take her. That lent an intimacy to their relationship she suddenly couldn't handle, especially when she thought about Stephen and his betrayal.

A neutral expression blanketed his features. "Sure. I understand."

Do you? she wanted to ask him but couldn't voice it aloud. She wasn't sure she understood all the conflicting emotions swirling around inside of her. She liked Peter—really liked him—too much. She wanted to get to know him better but was afraid of what could happen. Three of her children adored Peter, the fourth one tolerated him in order to be around his animals. She had no doubt, though, that somehow Peter would reach Sean in time. She'd seen how effective Peter was as a principal.

In another month Stephen would have been gone for a year. Even after all that time he still controlled her life as he had when he was alive. Fear held her back, and she wasn't sure she would ever let that go. She touched her cheek. The memory of the sting of Stephen's hand across her face still hurt. The bruises on her skin had faded but not the ones in her heart.

Chapter Six

Cara, I know you've been wondering when I would take Peter's offer up about going to church. Well, I did it! I took the children and went today. It helped that Aunt Sarah went with us. And I can't lie to you. It helped that Peter was there and made us feel so much a part of the congregation. In fact there were a lot of people I know that attend the Faith Community Church. They all made me feel as if I had come home.

But to be honest I don't know how I feel right now. I enjoyed the sermon. The words comforted me. And certainly the kids had fun, even Sean. The youth group is planning how to run the Shepherd Project, the name they gave Peter's undertaking with the animals. Sean actually contributed his opinion and I saw him talking with Chad. When I approached, I heard them discussing the two lambs they helped deliver. They both seemed like proud papas.

I'm praying for Mason and you. I'm glad he's back home from the hospital although I wish the doctors knew what was going on with him. My love and prayers, Laura.

Laura closed down her computer and stared at the black screen. Would her prayers help her friend's husband get through his illness? She wished her faith were as strong as Cara and Peter's, but then neither one of them was responsible for a person dying.

How can the Lord forgive me?

Why of all days did I agree to meet with Peter today at Noah's restaurant?

That question plagued her as Laura drove toward the place. Since she'd awakened this morning, her thoughts had been centered around the fact this was the first anniversary of Stephen's death. She might have been able to shake it off if Alexa hadn't said something about it at breakfast. She'd wanted to do something for her father, but since the grave site was in St. Louis, visiting it wasn't an option. Her daughter had asked her if she had any ideas what she could do. She didn't.

It was only one in the afternoon, and she was tired. Bone tired. She rarely took a nap, but that was all she wanted to do. The horror of those last few days of Stephen's life came flooding back, bringing with it all the pain she had gone through.

Laura pulled into the parking lot and brought her car to a stop. She needed to get out, but for the life of her she couldn't seem to open the door. The sound of the slap that had rocked her so hard that she had teetered at the top of the stairs, then plunged down them echoed through her mind. She shuddered.

Gripping the steering wheel, she laid her head against it. She had been so thankful the kids hadn't seen what had transpired between Stephen and her at the end. She'd been able to attribute her bruises to the fact that she'd fallen down the stairs. She would never have been able to explain their father's behavior.

A tap at her window startled her. Gasping, she twisted around to face Peter. He bent down to look into the car. She sucked in a calming breath that barely inflated her lungs and opened her door. With trembling legs she stood, clutching the vehicle for support.

"What's wrong?"

The concern in Peter's expression touched the coldness about her heart. "This wasn't a good idea."

His hand covered hers on the door. "Did something happen to one of the kids?"

She shook her head, unable to speak. Peter needed some kind of explanation, but she couldn't bring herself to tell anyone what Stephen had done that last day. She felt so ashamed that she had allowed it to happen.

Peter pried her hands from the door, leaned in and snatched her purse off the seat, then tugged her toward his truck. She didn't object even though a weak protest was stuck in her throat. Inside his blue Chevy, Peter switched on the engine.

That action prompted her to ask, "Where are we going?"

"Somewhere quiet and near."

Weary, she let him drive from the restaurant without

a protest. Finally when he parked next to the high school stadium, she angled toward him and asked, "Why here?"

"No one is here and it was near. I couldn't think of anywhere else nearby. The park is full of people so it was out."

"There's so much I need to be doing at home. Aunt Sarah has finally decided on a color to paint the house. It's actually very pretty, a forest-green. That should go well with the dark red brick. I need to get the supplies. There's nothing at the house. We start this weekend." The words tumbled from her as if she were a runaway train and couldn't stop them.

The anxiety in his gaze warred with the rest of his features, fixed in a neutral expression.

His look prompted her to add, "I should just go home. We can reschedule this another day."

"We could, but it wouldn't solve your problem."

"I don't have a problem."

One of his eyebrows rose. "Please, Laura. I've gotten quite good at reading people. You have to if you want to stay on top of what's going on with teenagers. They're sharp and hard to fool—like me."

She couldn't see any way to get out of telling Peter at least a little of what was bothering her. But she couldn't tell him the whole story. "This is the first anniversary of my husband's death."

"Oh."

That one short word held a wealth of meaning in it. It urged her to say more.

"If I can help—"

"Alexa wants to do something for her father but the grave site is in St. Louis—eight hours away. Any suggestions?" Desperation drove her to ask him. That and the fact that his expression coaxed her to believe he was different, that he would understand all her insecurities, the guilt she carried in her heart.

"Have her write in a journal. That can be very therapeutic. Maybe she could even write a letter to her father."

Laura knew how therapeutic her correspondence with Cara was for both her and her friend who was dealing with her husband's mysterious illness. Sharing their troubles made them seem bearable. "That's a wonderful idea. I should have thought of that. How did you get to be so smart?"

He actually reddened. She suddenly wanted to brush her fingers across his cheeks.

"C'mon." Peter pushed his door open. "We need to enjoy this mild day. Before long we'll be faced with over a hundred-degree days and no rain in sight."

She didn't move until he rounded the front of his truck and stood waiting for her, not an ounce of impatience on his face, as if he had all the time in the world to hang around until she decided what she wanted to do. Instinctively she knew that if she wanted to go home he would take her. That made it possible for her to open her door and climb from the cab.

He unlocked one of the gates and stood to the side to let her enter first. He pocketed his keys. "One of the perks of being the high school principal."

"A perk? You're easy to please."

Peter led her toward the nearest player bench on the west side of the field. "Actually, this place holds a lot of memories for me."

The early-afternoon sun, almost directly overhead, bathed the grass in bright light. "You played football?"

"Don't sound so incredulous. I was the kicker. It got me a college scholarship. Without it I don't know how I would have gotten to go to college." He sat and patted the wooden bench next to him. "But that's not why this place is special to me. I used to come here a lot in high school to think. I still do."

She eased down near the other end, afraid if she sat close she would tell him secrets she'd kept locked away. "The football stadium?"

"It's perfect. It's usually deserted, and chances are I'm not going to be bothered."

"How'd you get in when you were in high school? Surely they didn't give a student a key." Tension stiffened her spine. This whole place with Peter was too dangerous for her peace of mind. *Leave before you share a part of yourself.* Her cautious side blared the warning.

He chuckled. "True. Sometimes it was open during the day back then. At night I had a gift of being able to open locks."

"Peter! You picked the lock!"

"It was a piece of cake. Easily opened. Actually, it still does." He leaned close and lowered his voice. "I think the powers that be knew about it but didn't say anything. The coach was a good friend of Paul's. He often worked with me on my kicking. He said a few things that led me to believe he knew I came to the stadium after hours."

His musky scent engulfed her as if it were reaching out to blanket her in a protective cocoon. His whispered words fanned her cheek, reminding her of other times when they had been so close that she felt his breath. But the scariest thing was that he'd shared with her a place that was important to him. Why did Peter's revelation make her feel special and yet at the same time panicky?

He straightened, giving her some space as if he sensed her inner struggle. "Sometimes I'd pretend I was in the middle of a game and the whole outcome depended on my field goal. Or I would actually pretend I was the quarterback throwing the winning touchdown in the last seconds. Playing football gave me an opportunity to belong to a team, to be a part of something."

Laura snapped her fingers. "I've got it! Sean needs to go out for the team."

"I think you're mocking me."

She grasped onto his teasing tone and forced a lightness into hers. "Oh, no, whatever gave you that idea?"

"The laughter I hear in your voice." He rose and tugged her to her feet. "C'mon. I don't want you to knock the game until you've played it."

"Then I can knock it?"

"Yes, but not to my face." Although his expression was serious, his eyes held a twinkle.

She followed him out onto the field and slowly made a full turn, taking in the empty stadium, the bleachers, the press box, the sidelines. The grass had recently been mowed and the smell surrounded her.

"I'll be generous and let you score the first touchdown. I'll be the quarterback. You, the receiver. Go down field, and I'll throw you the imaginary football."

Suddenly she experienced a sensation of traveling back to when she had been a cheerleader and Stephen a pass receiver. She hadn't thought about that time in years. They had been the "perfect" couple in high school—voted most likely to end up together and have a wonderful life. Yeah, right, she thought—as tears she hadn't been able to shed since his death tried to fight their way to the surface. She swallowed over and over, trying desperately to keep them inside.

Peter loped out to the fifty-yard line, but she couldn't move. He turned toward her. When his gaze took her in, he covered the space between them at a jog and grasped her arms in a gentle hold. "Are you all right?"

She saw his concern through a sheen of tears. *Don't cry. Don't cry.*

"Laura? Did I say something wrong?"

Don't cry. But tears slid down her cheeks. She could taste their saltiness; she could feel their wet tracks.

"Ah, I'm sorry if I did. Don't cry, Laura."

Tears continued unchecked as memories tore down her composure. Peter drew her against him, stroking her back with long, even caresses. The emotions held at bay for months flooded her and she couldn't stop crying. One part of her was alarmed at how comforting and wonderful his embrace was while the other didn't care.

She drew strength from his arms about her. For just this one time she needed his strength.

What did I do wrong to make my husband hit me?
How could I have made my marriage work?
Why do I feel as though I killed Stephen?

Those questions crashed through her mind with no answers. They produced more tears until finally she had none left.

When she pulled back, staring up into Peter's face, the sadness in his eyes almost made her cry again. With a supreme effort, she reined in her emotions, swiping her hands across her cheeks. Embarrassment bubbled to the surface. "I'm sorry. I don't usually do that."

"You must have loved your husband a lot."

She couldn't lie to Peter, and yet she couldn't tell him that she had stopped loving Stephen that last year of marriage when his verbal attacks got more frequent. His words had undermined everything she had believed about herself and now she was struggling to find the person she was.

"Until I got out on this field, I hadn't thought about when Stephen and I were in high school. He was on the football team and I was a cheerleader. We both spent many Friday nights in a stadium. We started dating our junior year and married six months after we graduated."

A shadow clouded his eyes. "I married young, too. But my marriage didn't turn out well."

She didn't correct his impression of her marriage because the words jammed in her throat. No one but Cara knew how bad her marriage had really been. And then, even her friend didn't know everything.

"My wife filed for divorce three years ago. We had problems like all marriages do, but I never thought mine would end in divorce."

A bond sprang up between Peter and her. His pain pushed hers aside, and she concentrated on comforting him now, taking his hand within hers, wanting to share what strength she had with him. "Why'd she want a divorce?"

His features darkened.

"I don't mean to pry and you certainly don't have to answer me. I'll understand if you don't. I—"

He put a finger up to her lips and silenced her words. A half smile graced his mouth. "I've worked my way through the pain. There are some things in life you just can't change and the fact I can't father children is one of them. Diana wanted a whole houseful of kids. I wanted that, too, but I couldn't give them to her. She's married again and has two children already."

The fact that he kept track of Diana made Laura wonder if Peter had worked through his pain. He might think he had, but it lingered and could be heard beneath his words. She saw it in the tense line of his mouth, the wounded look in his eyes. She tightened her hand holding his, wishing she could draw his hurt into her. "You could have adopted. There are other ways to have a family."

"Not in Diana's mind. The bottom line was our marriage wasn't strong enough to weather the storm. Now that I've had time to examine it with some distance, I realize we had grown apart. I was willing to go into counseling, to work on it. She wasn't."

She took a step toward him. "I'm so sorry, Peter, especially about not being able to be a father. You would make a wonderful one."

Sadness eclipsed all other emotions visible in his eyes. "I never knew my own father, but Paul was an excellent example." He wrapped his other hand around their clasped ones. "You haven't met Alice yet. I wanted to introduce you two at church, but she's been sick and hasn't been able to go lately."

"I'm sorry to hear that. Is she okay?"

"She has diabetes and it gives her trouble from time to time. This morning when I called her to check on how she was doing, she told me she's back to normal. Has been for the past few days. I was going to pay her a visit this afternoon. Want to come along? You'd like her."

She did need to get the supplies so she and her children could start painting the duplexes. But at the moment she didn't want to be alone with her memories or thoughts. And maybe her presence would help Peter. This visit to the stadium had stirred up the past for both of them. "I've heard so much about her. I'd be honored to meet her."

He released her hand and inched closer. Brushing his thumbs across her cheeks, he said, "I know my divorce isn't the same as your husband dying, but time will heal your wounds."

Again his musky scent surrounded her as though he had the ability to enclose her within a protective shield where nothing could hurt her. He leaned forward slightly. Her pulse sped in anticipation of— what? A kiss?

Disconcerted at where her thoughts were taking her, Laura stepped back, pasting a smile on her face. "I know."

"Let's go see Alice." Peter headed across the field toward the gate.

"What about the fund-raiser?"

"We can talk another day or later after we pay Alice a visit. Frankly I've loved everything you've come up with and can't imagine me making it any better."

His compliment swayed her heart to surrender to his charms. But she couldn't emotionally afford another mistake. She had her children to think about as well as herself. She couldn't go through a relationship like the one she'd had with Stephen ever again. And from listening to Peter, she was beginning to realize he felt the same way about his marriage to Diana. Two wounded people, too afraid to trust. What a pair!

"Planning parties isn't my thing." Peter paused in their trek to the parking lot.

She laughed, a bit shaky, but she was desperate to get some lightness into the conversation. "So, Mr. Stone, just what is your thing?"

"Kids and animals." Starting forward, he threw her a glance over his shoulder. "I'm getting quite good at raising different kinds of animals thanks to our FFA teacher and the vet."

"Any new ones this week?" Laura passed through the gate and walked to his truck while he secured the padlock.

"A parrot that squawks all the time."

"Teach him to talk and maybe he won't squawk."

Peter slid behind the wheel and started the engine.

"He doesn't seem to want to learn any words. Frankly I can see why his former owners got rid of him. I came downstairs yesterday morning and his screech surprised me so much I dropped my cup of coffee. The mug shattered all over my tile floor. What a mess. Not to mention all the coffee that spattered over everything, staining it."

"When did you get him?"

"Two *long* days ago. Believe me, I won't forget he's in the house again." Peter pulled out of the stadium parking lot and turned onto a main street.

Fifteen minutes later he switched off his truck in front of the three-story white brick apartment building where Alice Henderson lived on the first floor in an older neighborhood of Cimarron City. Large oaks stood sentry on either side of the walk that led to the wraparound porch.

Peter paused on the top step. "I've been worried about Alice ever since Paul died. Their marriage was so strong that when he passed away I think he took a part of her with him."

Her parents' marriage was like that. They had made it look so easy. *Was that why I never went back home after Stephen died?* She couldn't shake the feeling that she had failed herself, her kids and her parents. It had been easier to come help Aunt Sarah than face her parents in Florida, knowing in her heart that her marriage falling apart had led to her husband's death.

Peter opened the front door for Laura. "Her health has suffered, but I can't get her to come live with me. I don't want her going into an assisted-living home. She took care of me when I needed it the most. I want to do the same."

"Independence is important to some people. Sometimes more than safety. I knew Aunt Sarah was really sick when she asked me to come help her."

"So it will take a crisis to get Alice to admit she needs help?"

"Possibly, and even then I don't know if she will."

"What happens if she doesn't ask for help in time?" Peter furrowed his brow.

"Then she lived her life the way she wanted." She understood so much better now. Standing on her own two feet was something she was striving for. Accepting Aunt Sarah's offer was a compromise. She hadn't been able to go it alone in St. Louis, but at the same time she wasn't running home to her parents and she was helping her aunt in the process.

"So it's better to be alone and autonomous than with someone who can help you?"

She looked him directly in the eye. "For some, yes."

Peter didn't have to be hit over the head with a two-by-four to know the conversation had shifted to Laura. What had made her want independence so much? She had told him about her life in St. Louis, but he suddenly realized it was only superficial facts, not really what her life had been like. Maybe her marriage hadn't been a good one. Or, so good that when her husband died, like with Alice's situation, he'd taken a part of her with him.

Peter rang the bell. "It takes her a while to get to the door. I have a key, but I don't want to use it unless it's an emergency. She wouldn't be too happy with me if I did."

"Maybe she's not home."

"I told her I was coming by. She's here. I hear the TV. She always turns it off when she's not watching. She knows how to save a penny better than anyone."

A minute later the sound of a bolt unlocking shifted Peter's attention to the door, which opened slowly. Alice peered around it, smiling. Her bluish-white hair styled in soft curls, rouge on her cheeks and a flowered dress proclaimed she had been ready for his visit. As he entered the apartment, he drew his foster mother into his arms and kissed her. Peter smelled her familiar rose scent. He felt as though he had come home after a long day at school and football practice.

"It's good to see you, Peter." Alice's sharp, lively eyes shifted to Laura. "And who is this?"

Laura came forward, sticking her hand out. "I'm Laura Williams."

Alice ignored the hand and instead enveloped her into a hug. "Any friend of Peter's is a friend of mine. Come in, you two." She swept her arm toward the neat, orderly living room.

On the coffee table were stacks of magazines, the Bible and lace doilies. The TV was still on, the volume loud because Alice was starting to lose her hearing.

She shuffled to her favorite worn lounge chair, eased down slowly as though each movement was painful, then glanced toward the television set in front of her, then to the remote lying on the coffee table out of her reach. She started to rise to retrieve the remote.

Peter waved her back down. "I'll get it for you. What are you watching?"

"I love this show. It's called *More Than Dreams*. It's

on every Wednesday night. I was at my Bible study last night and had to tape it." She took the remote and clicked the television off.

"I've seen that show a few times. It is good." Laura sat on the brocade couch.

Alice's brown eyes danced with merriment. "I love seeing those people's dreams come true. This last one was about helping a man and his family get the business he'd dreamed of having all his life. He was always helping others so it was nice to see someone do something for him."

"Do you have everything you need? Can I take you anywhere?" Peter settled next to Laura, noticing the tired lines on the older woman's face, the hand that shook.

"I'm fine. I have plenty of food to eat, my Bible, lots of magazine and books to read and my television shows. What more could I want?"

People. You're alone too much, but he wouldn't say that since they'd had this discussion before and Alice had made it clear she didn't need a parade of friends visiting. He was sure that wasn't the real reason because she'd always wanted and welcomed a houseful of others while he had been growing up in her home. "I'm a phone call away if you think of anything or you just want to talk."

Alice tsk-tsked. "Peter, I can entertain myself. Don't worry about me. I've been taking care of myself for fifty-five years—" she glanced at Laura "—because I don't count the first twenty." She winked. "Peter has mentioned you're helping him with the foundation he wants to start."

"I'm planning a fund-raiser for the second Saturday in September. It's gonna take quite a bit of money to make this work."

"But such a worthy cause." Alice swung her gaze to him. "How's the paperwork coming on setting up the foundation?"

"Tedious but necessary. A lawyer donated his time to help me with it. We've gotten our federal ID number and we are slowly moving forward."

"That's all you can ask for." Alice lifted her left leg up onto the ottoman in front of her. She winced and tried quickly to cover up the fact that she was in some pain. "Peter, can you be a dear and get us some iced tea? I have some made in the refrigerator."

Peter rose, wanting so bad to help her pack her bags and bring her to the ranch instead. He kept those words to himself, though, and said, "Sure. Do you want anything else?"

"No, dear. But I baked some chocolate chip cookies after you called."

"You aren't supposed to have cookies. I'd better relieve you of some."

Alice laughed. "Laura, that really means he'll clean me out of house and home. Nothing has changed in twenty years. Peter has such a sweet tooth, especially when it comes to chocolate. I can't blame him. I used to have one before I got diabetes."

He walked over to her, bent forward and kissed her cheek. "I only love your chocolate chip cookies. No one else makes them as good as you do."

"Why do you think I made them this morning?

Now go. I'm parched." Alice cupped her hand over her throat.

She waited until Peter left the room before shoving herself forward in her chair and leaning closer to Laura, motioning her nearer. "I didn't want to say anything in front of Peter, but I think I've got a way to get those homes built."

Laura closed the space between them by sitting on the sturdy coffee table. "How?"

"I think we should apply to the *More Than Dreams* show to build the homes."

"Homes? Peter is talking about one."

"That just it. If the show helps, he can have more than one. Who knows where this could lead? A whole community for the kids."

Laura saw where Peter's enthusiasm came from. "I'm willing to help. What do you want to do?"

"Can you go online and find out how to apply? Then you and I can fill out the application. I don't want to say anything to Peter until the show says yes." She winked. "This will be our little secret. I love surprises."

Left unsaid was the fact Alice didn't want to disappoint Peter if the show turned down the request. "I see why he thinks so much of you."

Alice reached over and patted Laura's arm. "My dear, I could say the same thing about you."

Pleasure warmed Laura's cheeks. She heard Peter leaving the kitchen and making his way through the dining room as if he were a herd of elephants. She scrambled back to the couch and pasted a smile on her face that probably shouted to him that she had become a coconspirator.

While Peter served the ladies glasses of iced tea and passed the plate of cookies to Laura, all she could do was wonder what Peter had told Alice about her. Her cheeks grew hotter as she contemplated what he might have said. What did Alice mean he thought highly of her? Laura couldn't get that question out of her mind as she nibbled on the delicious cookie. Before long she took another one, and when Peter announced it was time to go, she grabbed a third.

When Alice laboriously placed her left leg on the floor then put her hands on the arms of her chair to hoist herself out of it, Peter passed his foster mother the remote. "Stay there. I can find my way out of here."

"Don't forget to take the cookies with you. All of them. You can bring the plate back later."

He kissed Alice goodbye, then grabbed the goodies.

The smile Peter's foster mother offered her sent a feeling of comfort through Laura. She hugged the older woman and whispered, "I'll get the application and call you."

When she straightened, Alice said, "I know that Peter will be back, but I hope you'll come visit, too. I just know we're going to be good friends." Then she winked.

"When's a good time?" Laura moved toward the entrance.

"Any afternoon except Fridays I'm here. You don't need to stand on ceremony." Alice winked again.

Out in the hallway Peter pivoted toward her. "Okay, what are you two up to?"

Laura jabbed her finger against her chest. "Me and Alice? Why do you think we're up to something?"

"I know Alice. She doesn't usually become a person's best buddy in fifteen minutes. Granted she's always been accepting and open with others, but all that winking? That only happens when she's hiding something. I remember when she had a surprise party planned for Paul. I saw her wink five times in one afternoon. At first I thought she had an eye problem."

Laura marched toward the front door of the apartment building. "Really, Peter. It's nothing." At least, not at the moment, she added silently. "I promise you, we're not planning a surprise birthday party. By the way, when is your birthday?"

"Huh?"

"Your birthday? When is it?"

"Not until August 22."

"See, that's over four months away. You have nothing to worry about."

"Still, why did she wink?"

Laura shrugged and stepped outside onto the porch. "Maybe she had something in her eye this time. You could always go back and ask her."

"Ha! She would have made a great spy. No one is going to get anything out of Alice unless Alice wants it."

"She reminds me of Aunt Sarah."

"They're friends. They've been going to the same church ever since I can remember."

"Speaking of Aunt Sarah, I'd better get home. The kids should be converging on the house as we speak, and I don't want her to have to watch them long."

"Can't Sean watch them?"

"He could but he's helping Chad."

"Really?"

Laura breathed deeply of the flower-scented air. "Yes, Chad called my son last night and asked for help on training his dog. Sean's done a wonderful job with Lady. I gather Chad's mom gave him an ultimatum. Train the dog to behave or she'll get rid of it."

Peter descended the steps to the walkway. "Your son does have a way with animals."

"I wish I could say the same with people."

"Maybe he and Chad will become friends."

Peter opened the passenger door for Laura. "Hey, I think you have successfully changed the subject."

She smiled. "My lips are sealed."

Chapter Seven

Laura sat next to Alice at her dining room table with the application for the *More Than Dreams* show spread out between them. "I think we've gotten everything filled out. This is the perfect solution for getting the house built in a reasonable amount of time," she said with a feeling of accomplishment. *I'm really doing something to contribute to Peter's project.*

"You mean houses." Alice took a sip of her iced tea.

"You're thinking big. I like that."

"I'm hoping the producers will agree and want to build two when they see the need there is for foster care housing that gives children more of a home environment."

"After touring the shelter this morning where the kids go when they are taken from their parents, I'm hoping so, too. The people at the shelter have good intentions, but my heart aches for those kids." To think Peter had stayed at that very shelter right after his mother had died and there had been no one to take care of him. A heaviness in Laura's chest squeezed her lungs. Thankfully he hadn't stayed long, but the shuffling from foster home to foster home had left a deep mark on him that she suspected even today colored how he looked at the world.

"If this doesn't get them, then I don't know what will." Alice tapped the paper closest to her. "I appreciate you helping me with it. I want to help Peter with this, but I'm limited in what I can do. I don't move as fast as I used to."

"I've got a secret. I don't, either. Four kids will do that to a person."

Alice chuckled. "I remember. We always had at least four or five foster kids in our home." She paused and looked at Laura. "Peter was used to having a lot of people around. I'm sure he gets mighty lonely out at that ranch all by himself. Too bad Diana couldn't see her way to adopting."

A matchmaking twinkle sparkled in the older woman's eyes, sending alarm signals out to Laura. "He told me he's asked you to come live with him, Alice. Why don't you?"

She shook her head. "Oh, no. I'm too set in my ways. He's young. He needs young people around, people *your* age."

Laura bit into her lower lip to keep from laughing at Alice's blatant technique.

"I never did like Diana. I know that isn't being very Christian, but I can't help my feelings. I saw right through her when he brought her to meet me. I tried to tell him, but he was in love and wouldn't listen. My heart broke when she left him and married another man as soon as the ink dried on the divorce papers." Alice shook her head, a frown wrinkling her brow.

"He says he's worked his way past the hurt, but I don't know that he has."

"He needs a good woman to erase Diana from his heart. He'll see that when he meets the right one."

I'm not so sure of that. I can't see myself being able to forget or forgive what Stephen did.

"My dear, would you like some more tea?" Alice gestured toward Laura's empty glass.

She rose. "Let me get us both some more. Can I get you anything else while I'm in there?"

"Oh, no, just tea. I'm really thirsty." Alice stuffed her hands into the large pockets of her loose-fitting dress.

Laura walked into the bright, cheerful kitchen with yellow and red accents and removed the pitcher from the refrigerator. Mostly empty shelves with a few plastic containers and a small carton of orange juice captured her attention. As she took note of Alice's meager provisions, she heard the older woman say something and hurriedly slammed the door as though she had been caught doing something wrong.

When Laura made her way back into the dining room, she filled Alice's glass then sat again next to her. "If you need me to go shopping or something for you, I can. I often go for Aunt Sarah. It would be easy for me to do yours, too."

Alice fluttered her hand in the air. "I have everything I need. There's only one of me. I don't have to have a lot." She patted her waist. "I've got to keep my girlish figure."

"When I came in, the man across the hall asked about how you were doing. Is there something I should know?"

"Ha! That old coot can't keep up with me. Besides, after being married to Paul for almost fifty years, he spoiled me for anyone else." Alice took a sip of her tea and leaned toward Laura. "Paul reminded me of Paul in the Bible. My Paul's conversion was just as dramatic. I was pregnant and went into labor early. I believed in Jesus, but Paul didn't. When I nearly died on the oper-ating table, he promised the Lord he would be His if I didn't die." Tears glistened in Alice's brown eyes. "I lived but our child didn't. I couldn't have children after that. But you know something good came out of that tragedy. We became foster parents to one hundred and fifteen kids through the years, and Paul became a Chris-tian. You can't beat that!"

"But you lost your baby. You couldn't have any more." There were times her children drove her crazy, but she couldn't imagine her life without them. Hearing Alice's story made her reassess her situation. A lot of bad things have happened, but there have been some wonderful things, too. Without Stephen she wouldn't have Sean, Alexa, Joshua and Matthew.

"It was a small price to pay for what I was given. Those one hundred and fifteen children needed Paul and me. If we'd had our own, we might never have become foster parents. I've learned not to question God's plan."

But I questioned, Laura almost blurted out. Maybe the Lord was trying to tell her to appreciate what she had and to make the best of it. She was reminded of the old saying about making lemonade when life hands you lemons.

The sound of the doorbell startled Laura out of her reverie.

"Can you get that for me?" Alice gathered the papers and stuffed them into a manila folder.

"Sure. Are you expecting anyone?"

Alice shrugged but didn't say anything.

Laura hurried to the door and thrust it open. Standing in the hallway was Peter, looking disheveled, his hair a mess as if he had run his fingers through it repeatedly.

"What's wrong?" she asked, concerned by his furrowed brow and worried gaze.

"I got a call from Alice. She asked me to come over. She just hung up after that, and when I tried to call back, it was busy. I came as fast as I could. Did she call you, too?"

"No, I've been here for the past hour or so."

Frown deepening, he entered the apartment. "Then she's okay?"

"Peter, is that you?" Alice called from the dining room.

"Yes." He headed toward the sound of her voice. "You took several years off my life. Why did you call?"

The bluish-white-haired woman smiled sweetly and patted the chair next to her. "Do I have to have a reason?"

"Yes—I mean, no. Just don't scare me like that." He sat where she indicated.

"Would you like some iced tea?" Alice took a long sip of hers.

"No, thanks. So everything is okay?" Peter examined his foster mother's face.

Alice placed her hand on his arm. "My dear, I've just spent a lovely time with Laura. Everything is fine. Quit worrying. Come sit, Laura, and tell me about some of the donations you've gotten for the auction."

"I haven't gotten a lot, mostly little items. I just started this week going around to the businesses and letting them know about the fund-raiser." Laura looked at the table and noticed there was only one chair left and it was right next to Peter.

"Hasn't Noah donated anything?" Alice shifted her gaze from Laura to the chair then back to her.

"Yes, he was the first person. He's given us what will probably be the big prize—a vacation for four to Disney World." She scratched her head, sure there had been a fourth chair earlier. Was she losing her mind or was this another ploy by Alice? As Laura took the only seat left, she glimpsed the fourth one right inside the kitchen off to the side. With a hand covering her mouth, she smothered a laugh. Definitely one of Alice's ploys.

"Ah, Noah is such a sweet man and so handsome." Alice got a dreamy look on her face for a moment. "And you, too, Peter. Earlier Laura and I were talking about the kids I had in my home. You know, dear, out of the one hundred and fifteen children I helped raise, all but seventeen are married. Paul and I never officially adopted any of the children because we wanted to be able to serve as foster parents to as many as we could. You should see the pictures I get at Christmas from my kids. So many of them have such beautiful kids which I consider my grandchildren." Alice pinned her with an intensity as though she were honing in on her target. "You have beautiful children, Laura. Don't you think, Peter?" Her sharp gaze shifted to him.

"Have you met her kids?"

"Not yet, but she showed me their school pictures. I'm sure those twins keep you busy."

"On more than one occasion," Peter answered, then realized the question had been for Laura.

Laura's smile slid across her mouth. "Yes, they do, as Peter mentioned. In fact, I'd better get home. We're starting to paint the house this afternoon, and I don't want them to get it into their heads to begin without me."

"Wise of you. You should have seen the mess Peter made when he painted the garage with Jacob. I think they had more paint on them than the walls. Paul had to step in and take charge." Alice pressed her fingers to her lips for a few seconds as though trying to contain her laughter. "And he ended up with more paint on him than the walls, too. What a trio they were. I think they played war or something."

"Our version of paintball." He stood as Laura did.

"Remember I can pick up some groceries for you when I go shopping for Aunt Sarah. Just let me know." Laura hugged Alice goodbye then strode toward the front door.

A hand on her arm stopped Laura before leaving the apartment. "What did you mean you can get her some groceries?"

Peter's touch kindled a spark that shimmered clear down to her toes. Staring up into his eyes, so intent, she realized she was getting in over her head. She took a step out into the hallway, her skin tingling where his fingers had been. "She didn't have much in her refrigerator. I offered to go to the store for her."

"So she's not eating properly?"

"I don't know that for sure. She insists that she's okay."

"Alice would be on her deathbed and she would say that. I'll have another talk with her."

"I know you care, but Peter, maybe you should back off."

His gaze narrowed on her face.

"Sometimes when you try to force an issue, the person will just dig in harder. I know something about wanting to be independent no matter what. Take it from me, she won't appreciate your interference."

He sighed, the intensity melting from his features. "I'll try. It's not easy, though, when you care about a person and you have to stand back and watch them make a mistake."

"That sounds like what a parent has to do."

He blinked, then a wry grin curved his mouth. "I guess our roles have been switched."

"Which means, she won't appreciate it."

"Okay, I'll do it your way. See you later." He turned back into the apartment and quietly shut the door.

The click resounded in the foyer of the apartment building, reminding her of a cell closing. But instead of her emotions being hidden away, they lay exposed and open for exploration. She was in big trouble if Alice ever teamed up with Aunt Sarah and combined their matchmaking skills.

* * *

"Mom, Mr. Stone is here," Alexa shouted from the front yard, alerting the whole neighborhood.

Halfway up the ladder against the house in the back, Laura peered down at her attire. Twenty minutes into painting and she had forest-green streaks down the length of her, probably much like Peter when he'd been a teenager. Remembering Alice's story generated a smile as Laura climbed down and started around the side of her duplex.

She literally bumped into Peter coming from the front. His strong hands clasped her arms and steadied her. For a brief moment all her thoughts centered on the feel of his fingers on her. She was sure the pleasant temperature of seventy-eight, so unusual for this time in June, soared into the eighties in a matter of seconds.

"What brings you by? Is something wrong with Alice?" *Is something wrong with me? I have no business being attracted to Peter.* Laura backed up a few paces, needing to breathe the fresh summer air instead of his enveloping scent.

"No, but not long after you left Alice insisted I bring her over to visit Sarah."

"She did?"

"I guess seeing you reminded her that she hadn't seen Sarah in a while."

Sure, you keep on thinking that, Peter. "Where's Alice?"

"Inside with Sarah."

Oh, no! What she'd feared earlier was transpiring probably as she and Peter spoke. Those two old ladies were plotting their next moves if the tingling at her nape was any indication. "I could have brought her over to see my aunt. Why didn't she say anything to me?"

"I don't know. I went into the kitchen to get her some more tea and when I came out she announced she needed to come pay Sarah a visit. By the way, I did check out her food supply. I'm going to the grocery store later whether she likes it or not."

The second Peter was out of the room, no doubt Alice was on her cordless phone calling Sarah, just as Alice had called Peter to come over earlier while she was there. "You know what Alice is up to, don't you?"

"You mean trying to fix us up? Yes. She's never been subtle. But I can't refuse her when she wants me to do something. She doesn't ask for much." His mouth quirked up in a grin. "Besides, I wanted to come over and she gave me a reason."

"You did?" Her question ended on a squeak as though she had seen a mouse scurrying about her feet.

He inspected the house. "Yes. This is a big project, and I've definitely improved since I was a teenager painting the garage." His gaze skimmed down her length, pausing briefly at each swatch of forest-green on her skin and clothes. "I think you need me."

Need him? Those words panicked her. She would not become any more dependent on him than she already was. She enjoyed his company way too much. She was letting him help her with Sean. That had to be all. "It just takes me a little while to get into the swing of things."

"Swinging may be your problem." His regard lingered on a particularly long slash of paint on her yellow shorts.

"Funny. Are you sure you want to ruin that outfit?" She let her gaze trek down him, much as he had done to her. Which proved to be a big mistake. His clothes fit him nicely—too nicely for her peace of mind. "Those jeans look pretty new to me," she finally said, her throat dry, her voice raspy.

He glanced down. "They are. I could help prep the house."

"Prep?"

"Caulk, replace any rotten wood, scrape off old paint where needed."

"I think I forgot a step."

"You think?"

His laughter filled the air and tempted Laura to join in. "Okay. I never said I was good at this."

"Where's Sean?"

"On the other side of the house, painting. Why?"

"I'll get him and we'll go to the store and buy the necessary supplies to prepare the house. No more painting until I get back."

She saluted. "Yes, sir. But what do I do in the meantime?"

"I'd take away the brushes from Joshua and Matthew first. The bushes in front look a little greener than an hour ago."

Laura rushed past him. "They weren't supposed to paint. I may not know how to prep a house, but I do know the damage those two can do with paint and brushes. Where's Alexa?"

"She went inside to call Mindy."

When Laura reached her twins, they were brandishing the brushes like swords and flicking paint on everything—the flowers, the grass, the bushes and even on Lady—but the house. "Stop right now!"

Joshua and Matthew froze. Amazed they had, Laura couldn't think of anything to say for a few seconds. When Joshua finally moved, she hurried toward them. "Give me those brushes."

She should have known better. They both plunked them into her outstretched hand, covering it and her forearm with green paint. Their eyes widened.

"Go around back and take off your shorts and shirts, then wash off with the hose. Take Lady and clean her up, too." As they started toward the side of the house, she hastily added, "And don't get into any more mischief." When they were gone, she shook her head. "What am I gonna do?"

"Leave it to me and Sean."

"No!" She was losing control of the situation.

"Why not?"

"This isn't your problem." She scanned the mess about her and had to laugh. Who was she kidding? She'd lost control before she had started. She didn't know the first thing about painting the outside of a house.

"Can't I help a friend? Sarah can't do this, and I'm sure living on a limited income as she does she can't afford to pay someone to do it."

"Okay. You've made your point. Get the supplies you need, but I'm paying for them. That's the least I can do."

His broad shoulders lifted in a shrug. "Of course. With you, me and Sean working, it won't take too long. Maybe a week working in the evenings and on the weekend. I don't think we need to worry too much about it raining. That hasn't been in our forecast for a while. This time next week you won't recognize the house."

She watched him go around and get Sean. After they drove off in his truck, she attacked the mess left by her two youngest. Most of it would have to be cut off, the grass, bushes and flowers. Then she went to check on Joshua and Matthew and thankfully found them following her directions.

As they stomped into the house, leaving Lady to dry outside in the fenced backyard, Laura trailed behind her twins to make sure they didn't get everything wet. She found Alexa still on the phone and motioned for her to end the conversation.

"You were supposed to be the one painting out front, not Joshua and Matthew." Alexa's sheepish expression and dropped head almost made Laura laugh. She sighed. "Don't let your brothers go back outside. I'm going over to see Aunt Sarah. I don't want another mess out front or, for that matter, in the back."

Laura headed for the other duplex. Peter's observation about Aunt Sarah's finances only confirmed her determination that she would get hers under control and move to her own place. Her aunt needed the income from renting the duplex Laura and her children were living in rent free.

She knocked then let herself inside. Voices from the

back floated to her, and she walked toward the sound. What she needed to make clear to the two ladies in the kitchen was that she and Peter were only friends and that was the way it was going to remain—no matter how her heart reacted when he was near her.

"Child, what are you doing in here? I thought you were going to start painting. Alice said Peter came over to lend you a hand." Aunt Sarah put her china cup down in its saucer.

"Yeah, you should help Peter. It'll get done twice as fast." Alice winked at her aunt.

She was in trouble if Alice had resorted to winking. What have they been concocting? "He and Sean went to get more supplies. I thought I would take a moment to come see how you two were doing and to make something clear."

"Oh, how sweet of you. We're doing fine, dear." Alice turned to Aunt Sarah. "You have a nice niece who has been very helpful to me. Today I tricked Peter into going by the post office on the way over here. He doesn't know I mailed the *More Than Dreams* application."

Her aunt giggled as though she were a teenager again. "It's our little secret. I won't say a word."

Laura crossed her arms over her chest and strove to put a stern expression on her face. "Aunt Sarah. Alice." When they finally looked at her, she continued in an equally stern voice. "Peter and I are just friends. Please don't get any ideas about there being something more going on between us."

Aunt Sarah smiled so sweetly Laura was anticipating sugar dripping out of her mouth shortly. "Sure, Laura, whatever you say."

Alice perked up. "I think I hear a truck door. It's probably Peter back. You'd better go help him and don't worry about us. We're catching up on gossip."

"I don't hear anything." Frustrated that the two ladies were ignoring what she'd said, Laura unfolded her arms and took a step farther into the kitchen.

Alice waved her hand toward the door. "Oh, I'm sure he's out front. He'll need your help."

Giving up, Laura spun on her heel and stalked back through the house and out onto the porch. For someone who was hard of hearing, it was amazing Alice had heard Peter come back. But there he was with Sean unloading the truck.

Sean was cooperating with Peter, but in her son's eyes Laura could see a wariness that had been there for a long time. Didn't the two ladies realize that, like Sean, she didn't trust easily—not after what Stephen had done to her? Her deceased husband had torn their marriage and family apart. She would never place herself in that kind of situation again.

Chapter Eight

Cara, I know. I know. I had no business asking Peter out to dinner. But after all the work he did helping us to paint Aunt Sarah's house, I had to do something special for him. The house is done today and it looks great, thanks to Peter.

It did take a little longer than he'd anticipated because he hadn't counted on Joshua and Matthew's special kind of "help." We only lost one gallon of paint—not even a whole gallon—when Matthew ran around the side of the house and right into the ladder Peter was standing on. Neither one of my twins ever looks where he's going. I think their heads are actually in the clouds.

Thankfully Peter wasn't too high up when he came tumbling down. He landed on a bush that cushioned his fall some. After that little mishap, Peter clambered to his feet, a bit more slowly than usual, limped to the ladder and put it back in place. I gave him my paint can then proceeded to clean up the mess while he finished his area. It was dark by the time we put the last brushstroke to the wood, but Peter was on a mission to have it completed today.

What amazed me, though, about the whole accident—and it really was one, everything is with my twins—is that Peter never yelled or got angry at Matthew. He laughed when he saw the paint dripping off the plants under the ladder. We have started a new decorating trend in the neighborhood! Our foliage matches our house—this must have been the reason I picked green. Anyway back to the point I wanted to make, Stephen would have screamed and screamed at Matthew. Come to think of it, with Stephen my twins would have been confined to the house until the project was finished, instead of being a part of it. They did fetch things for us, helped with the cleanup and mostly stayed out of trouble. What more can a mother ask for?

I know you wanted me to tell you something funny and lighthearted, but I have to ask how Mason is holding up with the treatment. Are the newest antibiotics working yet? I continue to pray for Mason. I hope the Lord is listening. Love, Laura.

With a heavy heart Laura sent the e-mail and hoped it cheered up her friend. In Cara's posts she was trying to be upbeat, but Laura knew something was wrong. She wished Cara could confide in her, but she, of all people, knew how hard it was to tell another person her problems. At least her friend had the Lord to talk to. That was important to Cara. Would it be enough, though?

Laura heard the doorbell and glanced at her watch. Peter was right on time for their—what did she call this? It wasn't a date. She didn't date.

The cooling evening breeze after a warm day tickled her skin as Laura made her way up the walk toward her porch. "I'm not gonna let you pay for dinner, Peter Stone. This was *my* treat." Still put out with the man, she threw him a look she hoped conveyed her feelings. "That was underhanded to arrange with the restaurant ahead of time to pay for it."

"Because I knew you wouldn't let me if I didn't do it that way. When a man takes a woman out on a date, he pays for it. Chalk this up to I'm an old-fashioned kind of guy."

Date? No, that wasn't what they had been doing! She was thanking him. That was all. Period!

"Alice taught me well, and if she heard you paid for the dinner, she would have my head. Do you want to be responsible for that?"

We were not on a date. She glanced down at her outfit, a black sundress with large turquoise, hot pink, lime-green and orange flowers on it. Granted it was one of her favorite dresses, and she had taken extra care with her makeup and hair, but this was not a date.

Peter paused at the bottom step, worry pinching his lips together. "Say something."

How could she when the word *date* had robbed her of her reasoning? She turned away from his penetrating gaze and studied the darkness beyond the porch light. "We went to dinner, not on a date."

Silence greeted her declaration.

She finally looked at him. Worry no longer lined his face. His expression gave no hint of his feelings. He was so good at that. "I'm sorry. I didn't mean—"

He raised his hands, palms outward.

She started to step back, the memory of Stephen the last time she'd seen him raising his hand to her invading her thoughts. But she stopped when she heard Peter say, "Yes, you meant it, Laura. No, this wasn't a date in the traditional sense, but it was a man and a woman going out, sharing a wonderful time together." He pointed at her then himself. "We've been skirting around our feelings for months now. I haven't pushed because you're as skittish as a yearling. But I think there's more here than merely being friends."

His words hung in the air between them. "I don't know what to feel. I didn't come to Cimarron City to get involved with a man. I once let you think that my marriage was a good one and that I mourned my husband's death. It wasn't and I didn't." She held her breath, waiting to see disdain take over his expression.

"I'm sorry."

There was no disdain, no questions about what had gone wrong. Surprise shook her composure. Whenever she had displeased Stephen—and she knew she had displeased Peter—she'd heard about it from her husband. His belittling remarks still needled her.

Peter slowly reached for her hand, and when she didn't pull away, he took it and urged her up the steps to the porch swing at the far end by Aunt Sarah's duplex. "When my marriage fell apart, it left me devastated. I couldn't figure out what I'd done wrong. I spent months beating myself up over it until I had to stop it or I'd be useless. It took Jacob, though, to make me see what I was doing to myself and the people around me. I hadn't told anyone what had really gone on with Diana and I needed to. Sometimes you can't do things alone." He angled around so he faced her. "Sometimes you need someone to listen to your problems. Not necessarily to give you advice but to be a sounding board. Laura, when you are ready, I'll be there for you. But if you don't want to tell me, I'll understand. Please, though, pray to the Lord. He can help you."

Tears choked her throat. Any anger she'd felt earlier toward this man melted at his declaration. Deep inside a small part of her wanted to blurt the whole story out to Peter. But old habits didn't die easily, and she just couldn't utter the words that she had been abused in her marriage, first verbally and in the end physically. She couldn't shake the feeling of shame when she thought about it. Why hadn't she been able to stop it? What had she done wrong?

"You can call me anytime, Laura. Day or night. There were some nights it was hard to make it through."

Her tears rose, flooding her eyes. Glad for the darkness that shadowed them, she blinked them away and wiped her hand across her cheeks. "I appreciate the offer," was all she managed to say before her throat closed up.

He allowed the silence to lengthen while she frantically tried to compose herself. All she really wanted was for him to take her into his embrace, as he had at the stadium, and hold her. Just hold her. She kept the wish inside and sat stiffly on the swing, her fingers laced together in her lap.

When he touched her, she gasped and jumped. He snatched his hand away. "I'm sorry I startled you. Are you okay?"

The strain in his voice, his actions, finally focused her on Peter. He started to rise. She grabbed his arm to stop him. She was becoming good at pushing people away. She didn't want to be alone with her thoughts. She'd been alone too long with them. "Please stay."

"Are you sure? I don't want to make you uncomfortable."

"It's not you." *It's me.* "I—" She swallowed several times. "Will you hold me?"

For a heartbeat he didn't budge, then slowly he drew her into his arms. She lay her head on his shoulder, feeling the rise and fall of his chest, smelling his now-familiar scent that calmed her almost as much as his embrace. Peace settled over her, and her eyelids closed.

"Mom! Mom, thank goodness you're finally home."

The anger in her daughter's voice jerked Laura up. The screen door slammed closed as she came to her feet. Words she uttered way too often tumbled from her mouth. "What's wrong?"

The second Alexa stepped into the circle of light Laura knew what was wrong and probably who had caused it. Her daughter had red, green, black and blue designs up and down both of her arms.

"Joshua and Matthew did this to me when I fell asleep watching TV. They used permanent markers! Those don't come off easily!"

Laura sucked in a deep breath that did nothing to calm her building anger. Exhausted mentally after her conversation with Peter, she didn't want to deal with her twins. But she had no choice. As a single mom there was no one else.

Alexa pointed toward the house. "They're in there laughing. They think this is funny. What if it won't ever come off?"

"Most of it will scrub off and the rest will wear off, honey. It won't last long. I'll be there in a sec, and I'll take care of Joshua and Matthew."

"You better or I will."

After the screen door slammed shut again, Laura heaved a sigh. "The twins should have been in bed." When Peter's chuckle peppered the air, she spun on her heel and glared at him. "It's not funny. Alexa is going to a birthday party tomorrow. Wearing a long-sleeved shirt in the summer isn't the usual style."

He rose, moving into the light from the window as he struggled to contain his laughter. "They're quite a team."

"Yeah. Instead of sleeping, they are concocting a scheme to make their sister's life miserable."

"Isn't that the mission of all little boys?"

"It is for Joshua and Matthew." Through her weariness she began to see the humor in the prank. Not that she would ever say anything to Alexa. "Still, I can't let them think they can get away with it without some kind of consequence."

"What are some things they hate to do?"

"Doing their chores, cleaning their room."

"Then have them do Alexa's chores for the time it will take for the markings to totally disappear."

"I like that." *Peter should be a father,* she thought, not for the first time. "They won't like that."

She strode toward the door with Peter following her into the house. Shouts from the kitchen quickened her steps. When she entered the room, she found Alexa shouting and squirting her brothers with a red liquid from a spray bottle as they ran around, giggling.

"Alexa! Stop!"

Red droplets covered her tile floor with a few dripping off her twins. Alexa's wet hair—Laura hated to think what had made it wet—hung down into her face.

Peter came up behind her and clasped her upper arms, squeezing them briefly, silently giving her support. "This, too, shall pass."

"I caught them sneaking up on me with this." Alexa brandished the bottle. "They put red food coloring in some water. They wanted to see if my hair would turn red."

Out of the corner of her eye, Laura saw her twins creeping toward the door. She rounded on them. "Don't you two move a muscle. Alexa, go on upstairs and clean up."

"But, Mom—"

"I'll take care of Joshua and Matthew." She forced a sternness into her voice as well as into her expression.

When her daughter had slunk from the room, Laura

stared at her boys for a long, long moment, daring them to move. Like statues, they stayed still.

"You will clean up this mess. I'd better not find one drop of red anywhere, and for your sakes you'd better hope nothing is permanently red. Then tomorrow you'll be doing all of Alexa's chores until there isn't any evidence of your artwork left on her arms and in her hair."

"Yes!" she heard Alexa shout from the hallway, then the sound of footsteps running up the stairs.

"Aw, Mom, we were just having some fun. There was nothing on TV—"

She cut Joshua off with a wave of her hand. "There is no excuse for what you two did. You should have been in bed. It's ten. Now clean this mess up, then go straight to bed. No detours."

As she left the kitchen, Laura heard her sons' grumbling and smiled. Good. Maybe they would think twice before doing something like that again. Who was she kidding? Matthew and Joshua weren't going to change anytime soon. They took constant watching to keep in line. The very thought exhausted her further, but this was so much better than a year ago when her twins had been scared to do anything for fear of Stephen's anger. Although he'd never gotten physically abusive with the kids, during the last year of their marriage, he'd begun to belittle them, too, no longer confining it to just her.

In the middle of the living room Peter tugged her close, brushing his fingertips across her forehead, smoothing her creases. "We need to get them involved with the Shepherd Project. They need an outlet for all their energy. There's still seven weeks until school starts after Labor Day."

Concentrating on his words, not his touch, she said, "I thought the project was going to be for older kids."

"No, for all ages. Whoever needs it. The youth group is coming to the ranch tomorrow to start getting things organized. I've arranged to take a few animals to Twin Oaks. I'm gonna have the kids run the program with the nursing homes and the preschools."

"Sean hasn't said anything about going to your place tomorrow. Did he sign up to do it?"

Peter nodded. "I think he's coming with Chad early so they can check on their lambs."

"He won't appreciate the twins being there."

"I agree but I can take them with me on Sunday afternoon to the nursing home, if that's okay with you?" Peter rubbed his hands up and down her arms.

"That's fine." The urge to snuggle against him over-whelmed her. She clamped her teeth together and with a supreme effort remained where she stood.

His eyelids slid half-closed. His look sent her heart hammering. So loud was it beating, she wondered if he heard its quickening pace. His fingers trailed upward and delved into her hair. Cupping her head, he brought her closer. His lips hovered over hers as though he was giving her a chance to pull away if she wanted.

Their earlier conversation intruded into her thoughts. What was their relationship really? Her mind declared only friends while her heart screamed much more. His breath tangled with hers as he lowered his head even more. When his mouth settled over hers, she didn't care what their relationship was or about the war raging inside her. All her senses centered on his gentle, coaxing touch, his clean, fresh scent, his taste of peppermint. His kiss rattled her to her core and awakened a feminine reaction that she had thought died with her husband.

He wound his arms around her and pressed her against him. Swept away, Laura met his response with her own. His strength surrounded her, tempting her with his safe haven. All she had to do was give in to what he offered and maybe she wouldn't be so alone.

A moment of sanity pricked her bubble. But would she be her own person? Would she come to depend on him as she had on Stephen? Look what had happened there! The need to end it grew, and she pushed away. Drawing ragged breaths into her lungs, she backed up a few feet.

"It's getting late. I'd…" She couldn't think of anything else to say.

"I understand."

Do you? Because I'm not sure I do. "Thank you for dinner. But next time I'll have to invite you here to eat. That way you can't pull a fast one over on me." *Next time? One minute I'm pulling away from him, then I turn right around and imply there's a future that has nothing to do with just being friends.*

"Mom, the kitchen is cleaned."

She smiled. "Duty calls."

"I can let myself out. I'll talk to you later." He hesitated for a few seconds.

She did, too. His gaze seized hers as though there was a link between them that couldn't be broken.

"Mom!"

Until her son shouted again. She blinked and hurried toward the kitchen. She didn't think she could write about this to Cara just yet. How could she put her feelings down when she didn't know what they were?

"Joshua, you're in charge of the rabbit, and Matthew, you'll have Digger." Peter led Bosco into the nursing home on a leash while the boys hugged their animals against them.

Laura took up the rear. "Don't squeeze them too tightly."

Peter let the twins go ahead of him into the rec room while he hung back with Laura. He was glad she had decided to accompany them today, not because he couldn't deal with her sons but because he wanted to see her whenever possible.

The other night when he'd kissed her and held her, he felt as if it was the most natural thing in the world, as though he had come home. There were a lot of obstacles in their way, and he knew that he might be setting himself up to be hurt again. He wasn't even sure if he should consider getting serious. His marriage had left him leery of his own judgment. It was hard to trust it when he'd been so far off base with Diana, so betrayed by her.

"Are you sure they should be holding the animals?"

Laura's question pulled him away from his thoughts. "No, but the cages are too big to bring inside."

"How about a carrying tote, like a cat's?"

"Let's see how this goes. If it doesn't work, then I'll have to consider purchasing some." He noted the boys heading straight for a circle of older people in wheel-chairs in the center of the large room. "But Joshua and Matthew still need to learn to handle the animals because the beauty in this is being able to hold on to and love the pets. That's kinda hard in a carrier."

"How did the planning session go yesterday? Sean didn't say much when he got home."

"For starters we're pairing kids from the shelter with members of the youth group. They'll help with taking some of the animals to day cares, nursing homes and hospitals. Also they'll help with the care of the pets."

Laura watched Joshua put the rabbit in a woman's lap. "How are they going to get to the places?"

"I'll drive some. I'm also recruiting volunteers. I know of several church members who have expressed an interest."

"I'll help when I can."

"Great." He looked toward Matthew who had given the ferret to a man, bent over in a wheelchair. Digger curled up into a ball.

Matthew grinned at his brother. "My pet is better than yours."

Joshua screwed his mouth into a frown. "No, it isn't!" He let go of the rabbit, still sitting in the lady's lap, and took several steps toward his twin.

The old woman's frail grasp on the hare slipped off, and it sprang from her. It hopped across the room toward the couch. Peter darted after the pet at the same time Joshua realized what had happened and pursued it to the sofa.

"You get at that end and I'll drive it out." Peter knelt and peered underneath the couch.

Before he had a chance to do anything, the rabbit darted out and raced around the rec room. Joshua gave chase. One woman shrieked while another giggled. The man who held the ferret grumbled there was too much commotion, but he grinned from ear to ear.

By the time Peter had the rabbit cornered by the piano, he was out of breath and seriously questioning his wisdom in bringing two seven-year-olds to the nursing home. With large brown eyes, the hare stared up at him as though gauging its chances of making it across the room to the wide-open door. Peter reached toward the panting animal. At that moment Joshua drove toward it. Peter's grasp came up empty as the rabbit headed for the hallway and freedom.

Laura blocked its escape and slammed the door closed. She scooped up the furry beast before it could turn and race in the opposite direction.

"We haven't had this much excitement in months," the woman who had held the rabbit said.

"Quite a show, young man," another lady added.

Joshua and Matthew took a bow as though they had planned the whole little episode. Several of the old folks clapped, and one yelled he wanted more.

"That's all we need. My sons encouraged to do more of that," Laura whispered when she came up to Peter.

Winded from his mad dash about the room, Peter breathed shallow gasps and leaned close. "Especially since it was an accident. I'm afraid next time it won't be. I had visions of us chasing that rabbit all over the nursing home."

"One way to get our exercise."

Peter crossed to the nearest resident and let her pet Bosco. "Next time we'll have to make some kind of provision so the animals don't run wild."

"That's easy. Don't take my sons."

The laughter that laced her voice spoke to him on a level that scared him. He could get so used to being a part of her family. But Laura sent off warning signals. Only lately had he really begun to see how deeply hurt she was from her marriage. Her husband had been gone just a year. He remembered how confused he had been that first year after his divorce. And until recently he had thought he'd put his divorce completely behind him. Now he wasn't so sure.

With Laura escorting her sons around the circle to make sure the animals didn't get away, they stayed another half hour. A few continued to request more antics so by the time Peter rounded everyone up and they headed for his truck, an idea began to form in his mind.

Settled in the cab, he switched on the engine and backed out of the parking space. "Anyone for ice cream?"

Two yells from behind him confirmed their next destination. Five minutes later, he pulled up to a store that sold mostly ice cream. "Let's go inside. My treat."

The boys were out of the cab in a flash and racing toward the building. At a more sedate pace Peter entered with Laura. Joshua pressed his face up against the plastic shield to get a good look at all the varieties while Matthew gave his order of a double-dip chocolate ice-cream cone. After Joshua told the cashier his more exotic choices of raspberry, lemon and bubble gum, Peter motioned for Laura to go next.

"After this afternoon I'm treating myself to a double-dip caramel sundae."

The eager expression on Laura's face rivaled her sons'. *Today has been a good one,* Peter thought and realized he looked forward to the times he was with Laura and her family. He felt alive, needed, as though the Lord had brought them into his life for a purpose.

"I'll have the same as her," Peter said to the cashier. "But add a healthy amount of chocolate syrup, too."

A few minutes later, he sat across from Laura at a table for two because Joshua and Matthew had selected a similar one and had proceeded to snicker and throw them secretive glances.

"Should we be worried they're plotting something?" Peter savored the first bite of his delicious sweet.

"Yes. They're up to something, and I have a feeling it's directed at us. They keep looking over here. We'd better be on the lookout. No telling what they will do."

"I can't be too angry with them. Because of your sons, I've come up with a great idea. We can take using the animals to entertain the kids and old folks one step further."

She slid her spoon into her mouth and sighed. "Nothing's better than this. I love caramel. I'd take it any day over chocolate." She took another taste before saying, "From that gleam in your eye, I'm almost afraid to ask. What's your great idea?"

"We're going to come up with a comic routine to entertain our audience just like today. There are some in the youth group who are into the theater at school and would be great. Brandon is a fine actor and class clown according to some of his teachers."

"We could even use a clown with the children's groups. This has possibilities."

"Then you'll help me?"

"Sure."

Her answer made his day. Working with her was so easy. She was efficient and very capable. "We've got the paperwork completed and turned in to the government. I've got a reporter lined up to do an article on the Shepherd Project."

"Sadie, Tory and I have had a lot of success getting donations for the auction. I'm feeling good about this."

"Yeah, isn't it amazing how this is coming together?" Peter finished his sundae. "It's a God thing how this has all worked out."

"Don't sell yourself short. You've worked hard. I know this is summer vacation, but you're at school almost every day then come home and put in long hours on getting the foundation off the ground as well as the Shepherd Project up and running. When do you sleep?"

He captured her hand near his and drew her full attention to him. "This would never have been possible without the Lord. He's giving me the inspiration and desire to make this happen." He brushed his fingers across her knuckles, enjoying the connection. "He brought you into my life and see what you've done so far for the foundation? I don't know the first thing about organizing a fund-raiser. You have quite a gift."

She lowered her gaze, patches of red spotting her cheeks, but she didn't pull her hand back. "You'd have figured it out. You're a smart guy."

"All things have a purpose. They may not always be our purpose. Look at today with the rabbit getting loose. They loved it. It will be a great addition to our program, and the kids will enjoy doing it."

"They say laughter is the best medicine."

"I know I like hearing you laugh." More and more she was laughing as well as relaxing and smiling.

For a fleeting moment he considered talking with Sarah and finding out what had happened with Laura and her husband. He'd thought the vulnerability he'd glimpsed from the beginning was due to the recent death of her husband. Now he didn't. Something else had happened. An affair? Some kind of abuse?

No matter how much he wanted to know so he could help Laura more, he wouldn't ask her aunt. Laura had to tell him in her own time or it wouldn't mean anything. And he wanted it to mean something. He wanted more from her. That realization surprised him. He'd come to realize Laura wasn't ready to become romantically involved with another and she might never be. But then the same went for him. Or so he'd thought—until recently.

Chapter Nine

Cara, I'm so glad to hear Mason is responding to his treatment finally. I've been worried as I know you have. I will continue to pray. I'm happy to hear Mason will be leaving the hospital tomorrow. I know how hard it is on all three of you with Mason being in and out of the hospital these past few months. Give him—both your guys—a hug for me.

Remember me telling you about how enraged my daughter was at her brothers for marking her arms while she slept? I wish I could sleep as soundly as she does? Well, you would think she would have scrubbed and scrubbed to get the marks completely off. This is six days later and she still hasn't really washed her arms like she should have—ever since she heard the boys had to do her chores as long as the markings stay on her.

I heard them plotting about jumping her and one of them holding her down while the other scrubbed her arms. I put a stop to that, but I had a hard time not laughing at their predicament. Maybe they will think twice before doing something like that again— or not.

On a more serious note I'm still trying to process the weekend with Peter. I can't believe I broke down with him a second time. What has gotten into me? Peter is becoming more than a friend, and I don't know how to change it back to the way it was because I can't see me getting serious about another man.

I missed the abusive signs with Stephen. What if I did that again? I can't put myself through that again nor my children. I know. I know. The signs were there, but hindsight is always twenty-twenty. Stephen was controlling. Things had to be his way or he got angry. I couldn't even work except in his business and then only until it got going. I didn't have a life outside the home, and Stephen wanted it that way. And I'm finding I like a life outside the home. It makes me feel I can stand on my own two feet. I'm still relishing Peter's words about how good an organizer and planner I am. Please pray I do the right thing. Love, Laura.

After hurriedly sending the e-mail, she scrambled to get her purse and head out to the car with her twins in tow. Alice had just called and said she needed to see her right away. Before she could find out what was wrong, Alice hung up. Suspicion lurked in the back of her mind. What was Alice up to?

Fifteen minutes later Laura pulled up in front of the apartment building only to discover Alice waiting on the sidewalk, tapping her foot impatiently. The second she saw Laura's car, she scooted toward it faster than Laura had seen her move.

"We did it!" Alice waved the letter in front of her. "*More Than Dreams* is going to build not one but two homes for the foster children. I received the letter today by special courier and they also called shortly afterward. Peter doesn't know yet. We're gonna tell him."

Laura slid a gaze toward Alice getting into the passenger seat of her car. "I'm glad we're officially on the board of the foundation or they might have contacted Peter first."

"The producer was so sweet. He gave me a number to have Peter reach him after we spoke with him." Alice turned around to her twins in the back and added, "Not a word to Peter when we get out to the ranch."

Both Joshua and Matthew said, "Yes, ma'am," at the same time.

"You, Laura, have such sweet boys."

Laura threw a wide-eyed look at Alice. "They have their moments." On more than one occasion she had caught her twins whispering and sending her and Peter furtive glances. *I'm afraid that Alice's and Aunt Sarah's matchmaking has definitely spread to my two youngest. I'm afraid to turn my back on them. No telling what they will do.*

"I'm so glad you could come pick me up. I want this to be a total surprise to Peter." A huge grin curved Alice's mouth.

Laura turned her vehicle down the gravel road that led to the barn. "Well, we're here."

"Are you sure he's at the ranch? It's Thursday and he's usually at school until two or three in the summer."

"He's taking a few vacation days. He had some things to do around the place before school starts again. I only dropped Sean off an hour ago. Peter told me he and some of the kids from the youth group had a lot of work to finish. They've received several more animals."

Alice tsk-tsked. "That boy doesn't know how to take it easy. Vacation means no work or at least more play than work."

"He's really thrown himself into the Shepherd Project and the Henderson Foundation. He told me once the foster home is built the kids staying in it will take over the project with the animals."

"You talk to him a lot?"

The twinkle in Alice's eyes told Laura to tread lightly with her answer, especially with two little boys in the back seat, unusually quiet, listening to every word. If she gave the woman any encouragement, Alice would be sending out the wedding announcements this week. "Although I've ended up heading the fund-raiser, I like to keep Peter informed of what's going on. This is his idea. The rest of us are along for the ride."

Alice chuckled. "Even back in high school he always had the big ideas. Why, I can remember—"

"Hold that thought." Laura loved hearing stories about Peter growing up, but she'd pulled up beside the barn and Peter was striding toward them.

Peter came around to Alice's side of the car. "What brings you all out here?"

"Help an old lady out of the car and I'll tell you." Alice motioned with her hand for him to open the door wider while she clutched the notification letter in one hand and her purse in the other.

As her twins raced toward the barn, Laura climbed from her car and rounded it while Peter assisted Alice to her feet. His gaze lit upon the paper in his foster mother's hand.

Curiosity took hold of Peter. "What do you have there?"

"A dream come true!"

The joyful glee in Alice's voice rang out, vying with the hammering coming from the barn. "Alice got a brilliant idea and today it paid off." Laura's own delighted excitement mirrored Alice's.

"With Laura's help I applied to that show—*More Than Dreams*—to build you the foster home you wanted on this ranch and they have said yes, not to one, but two! This is a blessed day!"

Peter's eyes grew round. "You did what?"

Alice thrust the official registered letter into Peter's hands. "They sent a letter as well as called me this morning. Read it. The head producer wants you to phone him as soon as you receive this. So come on. Let's go up to the house and make that call." She tugged on Peter's arm.

His eyes even rounder, Peter looked up from reading the letter, shaking his head. "I don't believe this. This has got to be a joke."

"No, it isn't. I would never joke about something as serious as this." Alice hooked her arm through his. "Besides, I talked to the sweet man."

Peter turned toward Laura. "You were in on this and you didn't say a word?"

She smiled. "It wouldn't have been a surprise if I had."

His shock transformed into wonderment. "You know what this means?"

"The money we raise in September can go toward staffing the houses and other things that will be needed." His awestruck expression was the best payment for her time filling out the application, Laura decided.

"The suspense is killing me, Peter. Come on."

He laughed at Alice's eagerness. "I can't leave the kids. They're finishing up making another pen for some goats."

"Goats! When did you get them?" Laura peered toward the entrance into the barn where her twins had disappeared five minutes before.

"These weren't left on my doorstep. The FFA teacher donated them to the project. Goats are good for petting. The younger children will enjoy them." He patted Alice's gnarled hand on his arm. "Let me see if Sean and Chad will keep an eye on everyone until I can get back. I know how much this means to you. Be right back."

"We'll come with you. I haven't seen the inside of your barn since all your animal additions."

"Alice, that's not a bad idea. I want to check on the twins and make sure they aren't getting into too much trouble. This past week they have been awfully quiet and well behaved." Laura strode with Peter and his foster mother into the barn's cool interior.

Sean pounded a nail into a board while Chad held it straight. The two boys chatted but stopped when they saw them coming.

"Hi, Mom. You weren't gone long. We have at least another two hours of work."

"That's okay. Where's Matthew and Joshua?"

Sean nodded toward the second stall from the end. "They're playing with the new puppies. We're gonna try to find them homes or at least most of them when they're older. Maybe we could—"

Laura hurried to cut off his request before the twins heard. "One dog is enough right now."

Peter scanned the area. "Where are the others?"

"They went on out to start working on the fence that needs repairing." Sean positioned another nail and drove it into the board.

"We're going up to the house for a while. If there's a problem, come get me. I'm leaving you in charge, Sean, Chad."

"You are?—I mean, great. Chad and me will finish up in here then help with the fence."

As Peter and Alice started for the entrance, Laura lingered. "Please watch out—"

"I know, Mom. Watch Joshua and Matthew. They won't do anything wrong. They know if they do they won't be able to come out here and help with the animals."

Since when had her son gotten so wise? Only a few months before he would have yelled at them and told them not to do anything wrong or else. As she hurried to catch up with Peter and Alice, Laura was struck by the revelation that Sean in the past had only been emulating Stephen. Now, though, he had seen how Peter interacted with people who had messed up. Peter didn't fly into a rage as her husband had. Peter dealt with most situations with patience and understanding.

So much in her family was changing and mostly because of the man next to her. She'd known Peter for almost five months, and his impact on her life left her facing the fact that she was probably in over her head.

The second they reached Peter's house, he went straight for the phone in his kitchen and punched in the numbers listed on the letter while Alice eased down onto a chair.

Laura held her breath while he was switched to the producer. Every muscle tensed in excitement as she watched Peter converse with the person on the other end of the line.

Thank you, Lord. Peter is a good man and deserves this. Better yet, the foster children deserve a good home.

Peter hung up, his hand lingering on the receiver, his stare fastened on the phone.

"Peter! Give us the details." Alice's raised voice brought him out of his stunned state.

"There was a part of me that even as I was waiting to be put through to Mr. McGraw figured this whole thing was a hoax." He swung fully around to face them. "It's not. It's going to happen the last week in August, less than a month away. We'll be one of the first shows on next season." He drew in a deep breath. "They decided to move a few shows around so they could slot ours early."

Joy sent Laura across the room and into his arms. She kissed him on the cheek. Then embarrassed by her impulsive reaction, she stepped back. "Everything is happening so fast." *In more ways than just the show building the homes.* She could barely grasp who she was becoming. Her feelings for Peter were quickly changing, evolving into something she wasn't sure she could handle.

"Yeah, Mr. McGraw told me that he was a foster child and he couldn't pass up this opportunity. He thinks the Henderson Foundation sounds great. A couple of the production people from the show will be here in a few weeks to start things rolling." Peter shook his head. "This is unbelievable and it wouldn't have been possible without you two."

"It really was all Alice's doing. She came up with the idea. I just helped with the application."

Alice's face reddened. "Nonsense. It was both of us."

Peter looked first at her then his foster mother. "I don't care how it came about. Thank God the kids will have homes months before I ever imagined."

"Amen." Alice lumbered to her feet, swaying toward the table. She clutched its edge.

"Are you all right?" Laura rushed to her side and grasped her arm to make sure she was steady.

Peter came up on Alice's other side. "Are you eating enough?"

"I'm eating fine. Whatever made you ask that?"

"I saw your refrigerator a few weeks ago."

"And you brought me some food." She tapped his chest with her index finger. "I'm okay. Quit worrying about me. We have too many other things to think about. A lot is going to happen in the next month."

Peter laughed. "And in the middle of all that, school will start."

"Oh, I hadn't thought about that." Out of the corner of her eye Laura caught something red flashing by the window. Matthew? He had on a red shirt. No, why would he be up at the house?

She walked to the back door and stuck her head out to see what was going on. She saw someone small wearing a red shirt ducking into the barn. It could only be Matthew. Her mother alarm went off.

"I think we should get back to the barn. Matthew is up to something. The back of my neck is tingling. That's a dead giveaway." Laura didn't wait for Alice or Peter but headed across the yard.

Inside the deserted structure she searched the shadows, but Matthew was nowhere to be seen. She strode toward the back and found all the members of the youth group working with both her youngest sons in the middle, helping, too. Thankfully, she overreacted—this time.

Several weeks later with coffee in hand Laura went out onto her porch to get the newspaper and nearly tripped over the vase of flowers sitting before the door. She caught herself before falling, but the hot liquid sloshed over the rim of her mug and onto her hand. She dropped her cup, and it shattered into tiny pieces all over the wooden slats.

Having been up late working on the fund-raiser, she tried to blink the gritty feel from her eyes so she could focus better on the array of multicolored flowers before her. But exhaustion clung to her like sweat on a hot, steamy day. She picked up the vase, examining it. A bright white card stuck out of the floral arrangement. She plucked it out, and setting the vase back on the porch, she read the cursive writing that looked familiar.

Laura, I wanted to give you beautiful flowers for a beautiful person. I'm hoping you and your children will go riding with me this evening. Peter.

Huh? This isn't Peter's handwriting. It's—she examined it for a moment—*it's Alexa's. Her daughter, too? Trying her hand at matchmaking?*

She didn't have time to ponder the question because the phone rang. She snatched up the vase and hurried back into the house to answer it. "Hello."

"Hi, Laura. This is Peter."

After the first word, she knew who it was. His deep voice was smooth and husky, very distinctive, and its sound made her smile.

"I'd love for you and your family to come out this evening and we can go for a ride. After all, we have something big to celebrate."

Puzzled, Laura studied the card again. It was Alexa's handwriting. She was sure. "Fine. They'll love it. It doesn't take any convincing to get them to go for a ride."

"Great. How about five? Afterward, we can order a pizza and enjoy the brownies you made for me. Thank you for thinking of me."

Brownies? She'd discovered Alexa, Joshua and Matthew yesterday morning making some. They'd said it was for a friend. She'd been so busy she hadn't questioned them. Next time she would. "I didn't make any for you."

"But the note said—"

"Did you put some flowers for me on my porch?"

"No, but that's not a bad idea. Someone sent you flowers?"

For a second she imagined she heard worry—or was it jealousy?—in his voice. "The card said they were from you. But I know who sent them."

"The twins?"

"They were probably in on it. Alexa wrote the card. She tried to disguise her handwriting, but the heart over the *i* was a dead giveaway."

His chuckle floated over the line. "A heart. Great touch. I'll have to think about using that when courting a woman."

Courting a woman! She felt her temperature rise. Words fled her thoughts.

"I still want you to come over. Five?"

"Sure. How about the kids?"

"Bring them. They went to a lot of trouble to make this happen. I would hate to disappoint them. If this is what they've been planning, let's give them what they want or there's no telling what they will do."

"Smart man. We'll be there, except for Sean."

"Oh, yeah. The lock-in at the church. Until then."

When she returned the receiver to its cradle, her legs suddenly weak, she sank back against the table in the living room. Well, at least with the kids there this wouldn't be a date. She could relax and enjoy the evening.

She straightened and decided to clean up the mess on the porch. But as she picked up the shards, they reminded her of her life when she'd come to Cimarron City—shattered into hundreds of pieces. Slowly she was gluing it back together. She'd found something she really enjoyed doing—Peter's foundation and fundraiser. Her debts were slowly dwindling with careful management of her money. Even not working for two months during the summer, paying no rent had really helped.

So why was she so worried about what was happening to her heart? Three of her children wanted to see her and Peter together—at least dating. That was obvious from their comments and their antics. And that was the problem. It was one thing if she got hurt if a relationship didn't work out between her and Peter, but if her children did… She couldn't risk that. They had gone through so much in the past year. Sean was still hurting, and she wasn't sure how he would feel about Peter "courting" her.

Lord, are You listening? Can You help me? What do I do? I really care about Peter, and he's great with the kids. But are they the reason he's always around? Does he see me as the means to that family he wants? If I ever wanted to get married again and that is a big if, I would want the man to marry me because of me. Stephen always tried to mold me into someone I wasn't. Peter hasn't, but then he still has some deep issues concerning his ex-wife. What do I do?

There. She had finally voiced something that had been troubling her. Did he like her company because of her or her family? Could he ever get beyond his wife leaving him to trust another? She knew she wanted that in a relationship.

When the phone rang a few minutes later, she half expected it to be Peter again. "Forget something?"

"Forget something? I don't understand."

"Cara!" Laura chuckled. "I thought you were Peter calling me again. What's up?"

"Mason's back in the hospital. He's had a relapse. They have exhausted all avenues here in St. Louis. They now think it's a fungus that isn't responding to their treatment. They're talking about sending him to the Mayo Clinic…." A long pause broken by a sob followed.

"Oh, Cara, what can I do? When will you all leave?"

"I—I don't know. He's in intensive care and the doctors are conferring right now. I had to call someone. I don't know what to do anymore. I—I…" Her voice trailed off into another sob.

"Pray, Cara. Mason is in the Lord's hands now." As she spoke the words to her friend, there was a part of her that was amazed she had said that. She wouldn't have a month ago, but she found herself praying more and more, as though it was the most natural thing to do.

"Yes. Yes, he is. It's been so hectic since bringing him into the hospital a few hours ago. I haven't had time, but you're right. I need to seek the Lord."

Laura heard voices in the background, then Cara said, "I've got to go. The doctors want to talk with me. I'll let you know what's going on when I know. Bye."

When Laura replaced the receiver in its cradle, tears smarted her eyes. Mason and Cara were so much in love. *Please, God, don't let anything happen to him. I don't know what my friend would do if she lost Mason.*

Later that day as Laura rode toward the stream, she thought back over the conversation she'd had with Cara—the second one—right before she had come to the ranch. Mason and Cara were going to the Mayo Clinic early the next morning. Arrangements had just been completed and Cara had wanted her to know. She heard the worry in her friend's voice and wished she could be there with her. But at the end Cara had assured her everything would work out. Laura hoped so.

Near the creek she dismounted her horse and tied the reins to a small tree nearby while Peter did likewise. Alexa, Joshua and Matthew followed suit, then huddled together.

Laura caught Peter's gaze and shrugged. "Sorry, they're never gonna change. I feel like I'm on a stage and they're the audience."

"We could always give them something to talk about."

Surprise shocked the words from her mind. Instantly a picture of them locked together in an embrace popped into her thoughts.

He chuckled. "G rated." He held out his hand to her.

She took it, trying to ignore the tiny bit of disappointment taking hold.

"Let's go for a walk and see if they follow."

"What are you up to?"

"Nothing really. I'm making them work for it. Besides, I'd like to show you a small waterfall I have on the ranch. It's nearby." He pointed toward the creek. "This originates in the hills on the west side of my property."

Five minutes later Peter stopped at a waterfall, crystal clear liquid tumbling over large boulders into the stream. An assortment of different trees shaded the small pool that had formed at the bottom of the hill. Very tranquil. Very romantic. Very secluded for a nice picnic away from…

He faced her, taking her other hand within his. His touch snatched the rest of the thoughts from her mind and all she could do was stare into his dark eyes and melt.

His half-lidded look bored into her. "I might not have written the card or given you the flowers, but I agree with what your kids said. Beautiful flowers for the beautiful person you are."

Compliments had always made her uneasy. The rare times Stephen had given her one he'd always wanted something in return and then later had taken it back. It had made her cautious about the motive behind one.

The sound of rustling behind her caused the corners of her mouth to lift. Right on cue her kids had followed them. She peered over her shoulder but couldn't see them. They must have been hidden behind the bushes off to the side. Oh, well, so much for secluded.

"Do you think any moment they are going to jump out at us?" He lowered his voice so it didn't carry, his eyes gleaming with silent laughter.

"No, probably Aunt Sarah and Alice instructed them in what to do. They're probably watching so they can report back to those two."

"Then we are in trouble."

More rustling drifted on the air. Laura pivoted. "Okay, you all come out here right now. The gig is up."

Nothing.

The noise grew louder as though an animal was crashing through the underbrush. Laura stepped back, coming up against Peter. "I don't think that's the kids."

The second she said that, a big dark brown dog loped out of the wooded area, chasing a rabbit from the bushes. As the hare darted past her and Peter, scurrying into a hollow log, the Great Dane skidded to a stop and barked at the hole where his prize had disappeared.

Laura pressed back into Peter, his hands clasping her arms. "Is this one of your new animals?"

"Never seen him before."

His whispered reply tickled her neck and made her shiver. "He's huge," she murmured, imagining her eyes were, too.

The continual barking drowned out the sound of the water flowing over the rocks. The Great Dane lay down and crawled toward the dark hole, sticking his nose into it. Blessedly it became quiet as the dog investigated.

"Occasionally dogs left out here roam around in packs. He may be a part of one. He looks underfed."

"Maybe we should get back to the kids. I'm surprised they haven't come to see what all the noise is about."

She and Peter in unison slowly backed away from the Great Dane. Laura held her breath until her lungs burned, afraid that any second the dog would turn on them. They had taken a half a dozen steps when the beast finally gave up on the rabbit and shifted his *full* attention to them.

The Great Dane stood, emitting a low growl.

Laura froze. "What do we do?"

"Keep moving away *slowly*. Try to show no fear."

"Do you think he's visualizing us as two large steaks?"

"Probably—and there's no hole for us to crawl in."

"How about a tree? I can scramble up one if I have to." Laura kept moving toward where her children were. If this dog was part of a pack, then where were the other ones? She was afraid to ask the question out loud for fear of the answer.

Five yards away the Great Dane barked several more times then trotted into the middle of the stream and drank.

"Let's go a little faster while his attention is elsewhere." Peter grabbed her hand and increased his pace, always keeping an eye on the huge animal.

When they were out of sight of the Great Dane, Laura whirled around and ran, praying her children were okay. Coming into the clearing where she and Peter had left the horses and her kids, she came to a halt. It was empty. No children. No horses.

"Where are they?" Sweat beaded her forehead. Panic-stricken, she swiped her hand across it and spun around toward Peter. "What happened here?"

"I don't know, but let's get back to the barn." Peter

threw a glance over his shoulder in the direction they'd come. "I don't want to be around if that dog decides to pay us a visit."

They started back, leaving the coolness of the woods. In the open meadow the sun beat down on Laura, covering her in a thin sheen of sweat. Her heart pounded a quickened beat with each step she took. Were her children all right? Did they flee because they saw a pack of wild dogs? Or something else? Until she knew the answers fear gripped her heart.

The barn doors stood wide open, beckoning them into the refreshing shade. Laura hurried her pace. "They better be here and all right."

But when she and Peter entered, no one was around. Its very emptiness sent alarm skittering down her.

He headed to the stalls. "The horses are here." Leaning over the top rail, he plucked off a note taped to the wood. "And I think I know where your kids are. This says for us to go up to my house."

She stormed out of the barn and across his yard. "Wait until I get my hands on them for scaring me. They set us up. Well, except for the dog." She glanced over at Peter. "At least I think the dog wasn't part of this whole matchmaking scheme."

His chuckle penetrated her anger. "Look on the bright side. They care about you."

She halted in the middle of his backyard, in sight of the patio table covered in a white cloth with dishes on it. Her chest rose and fell rapidly. "I prefer they stop their meddling and that includes Aunt Sarah and Alice.

I can do just fine on my own." She started for the deck, hoping she sounded convincing because she wasn't really sure she could do fine on her own—not when it came to dating. She'd never dated much and what little she had had been over seventeen years ago.

"They had help, the adult kind." Peter gestured toward the nice dishes, the silver candlesticks with long white candles in them, the silverware and white linen napkins. "Those look suspiciously like Alice's." He pointed toward the crystal stemware.

"And the candlesticks are Aunt Sarah's. I've seen them in her china cabinet." Laura picked up an envelope with their names on it and opened it. "Enjoy the delicious meal, courtesy of us." She turned over the note card. "There's no signature, but this is definitely Alexa's handwriting. I'm not sure those are her words or the twins', though."

"More likely Alice's or Sarah's. Alice doesn't drive, but Sarah does. She must have come out here and set this up with Alice's help then taken the kids back home."

"Where's the delicious meal?"

One of Peter's eyebrows rose. "In the house? Alice has a key."

Inside the kitchen another note directed Peter to the oven where a chicken casserole sat on the middle rack. "At least they signed this one so we know for sure your children are okay and involved in the plot."

Laura removed the tossed green salad from the refrigerator. "There's a French silk pie in here."

"Alice can't have it anymore, but she used to love to

make that and I loved to eat it. My mouth's watering just thinking about it. Do you want to retire to the patio and enjoy the fruit of their labors?"

"We shouldn't let good food go to waste." She cradled the wooden salad bowl against her chest and grabbed two different dressings, ranch and raspberry vinaigrette.

"They went to a lot of trouble." Holding the casserole, Peter let her go outside first.

She needed to talk with her children. She wanted to make it clear she didn't want their interference. She was afraid they would get their hopes up and be disappointed and hurt. From some of Peter's comments she didn't think he was ready for any kind of lasting commitment, either. And that was the only kind she could be involved in—that was if she ever decided really to date again.

Peter held Laura's chair out and she sat, saying, "This isn't quite how I envisioned dinner tonight. A far cry from pizza."

"Don't let Noah hear you say that. He thinks pizza is the ultimate food."

"Well, if I owned a chain of pizza restaurants, I would, too."

Peter poured ice water that had been sitting in a silver pitcher on the table into their crystal glasses. "I worry about him."

"Why?"

"On the surface he looks like he's on top of the world, but I'm not convinced he really is. He works hard and plays hard as though there's no tomorrow. He's running away from something and I'm afraid it will catch up with him one day."

Laura spooned the chicken dish onto her plate. "When it does, you'll be there as his friend."

"I'm not sure he'll let me help him. I've tried and he won't listen."

"Maybe he's not ready. You can't help a person unless they are." She knew from experience. "For some it isn't always easy to accept help."

"We all need help. No one can stand totally alone."

"But we can't always depend on others to rescue us, either."

His gaze trapped hers. "Do you need rescuing?"

I did once and for the longest time didn't really know it. "I'm doing fine. My family is adjusting to Cimarron City. Sean seems happier. I like my job. I'm paying off some bills. I enjoy working on the fund-raiser."

His eyes narrowed on her face. "Then why don't you sound more convincing?"

She looked away, across the yard. "I have some problems I'm still trying to work through." The second she said it she bit down on her lower lip, determined not to reveal any more.

"I'm a good listener. If you need a sounding board, just holler."

She turned back to him, surprised by the sudden lightness in his voice.

"I know when not to push. You aren't ready."

"I did receive two calls from Cara today. You know my friend who lived next door to me in St. Louis. Her husband is back in the hospital and they have decided to send him to the Mayo Clinic tomorrow morning. It doesn't sound good. The doctors haven't been very successful in treating him."

"I'm sorry to hear that, but he hopefully will get the help he needs."

"I hope so." Laura stared across the yard toward the barn. She had to put Mason's situation in God's hands, and if something happened, she would be there for her friend as much as she could be.

Peter laid a hand on her arm. "You?"

She turned back to him. "Yes, just thinking about Mason and Cara. It's hard not being there with her, but I can't leave my family."

A pensive expression darkened his eyes. "Sometimes we can't do what we want to do. That's life."

What did Peter want to do that he couldn't? Have children? Something else? "The next month or so will be a whirlwind with the start of school, the *More Than Dreams* show and the fund-raiser. I'm here if you need to talk. I'm a good listener, too." He tried to present a brave front to others, but she'd seen his pain and vulnerability beneath the surface, especially more and more as she got to know him better. He, too, was good at hiding his true feelings behind a facade.

His mouth tilted up in a lopsided grin. "You might regret offering. By the time I get around to being able to talk, it will be the middle of the night. Are you sure you're willing to listen then?" A twinkle gleamed in his eyes.

Her heartbreak kicked up a notch. "A friend doesn't put a time constraint on a friendship. If you need me in the middle of the night, you have my number."

His look drilled into her, and a connection leaped across the table as though she'd been zapped with a bolt of lightning. He started to say something, shook his head and brought his fork to his mouth.

Laura watched him eat for a moment, her stomach knotted with her conflicting emotions. She wanted more from their relationship, yet she was afraid of more.

Lord, what do I do? Can You help me this time? Or am I alone?

No one can stand totally alone. Peter's words came back to haunt her. *Are You speaking to me through Peter, Lord? I depended so much on Stephen that I didn't even see how harmful his verbal abuse was to me and my children until the damage nearly destroyed me.*

"Laura, we have a visitor."

She twisted around and saw the Great Dane trotting toward them. She stiffened, gripping her fork. "What do we do? Do you think he smelled the chicken?"

"Thankfully Bosco is in the house."

"Maybe he isn't a part of a wild pack. Maybe he's seeking a home." *Like me.* Suddenly the tension left her as if God had placed his hands on her shoulders and whispered, "I am here for you."

She relaxed in her chair while Peter scooted his back and rose. He went to a large box at the far end of the patio and lifted its lid. After pulling out a bag of dog food, he took a large bowl then headed to the steps.

The Great Dane stopped at the bottom and looked up at them with sad eyes. Peter descended and placed the metal container on the ground then filled it. The huge beast stuck his head in the food and ate.

"You've got a new friend." Laura stood. "It's getting mighty crowded."

Peter's whole face lit with a smile. "We'll make room. I always have a home for someone in need."

All you have to do is take a risk, Laura. The thought was tempting, but she didn't know if she could.

Peter lifted his head and glanced toward his back door. "That's the phone." He hurried inside.

That left Laura with the huge dog. She thought about slowly making her way toward the house, but its tail wagging stopped her.

"Maybe I should take a risk and stay here with you, buddy." Although she didn't move, she kept an eye on the Great Dane as he devoured the dog food.

"Laura, the phone's for you." Peter handed her his mobile one. His frown alerted her that the call wouldn't be a good one. "It's Cara. Your daughter gave her my number."

"Laura, I—I wanted—"

The roughened tone to Cara's voice told Laura that something was very wrong. She sank down onto her chair. "Is Mason all right?"

"He died a while ago. I—I don't—" Tears drenched her friend's words.

"I'm coming. I'll be there tomorrow just as soon as I find somewhere for my children to stay."

"Hurry."

When Laura clicked the phone off, she let it drop into her lap, numb, her mind blank. Peter plucked it up and placed it on the table, then drew her to her feet. He took her into his embrace and held her.

Then the tears came. She cried for Mason. She cried for Cara. She cried for their son. In all the years she'd been married to Stephen she'd never felt she could show her emotions as she had with Peter. What would she have done without him standing here?

When she stepped back, putting some space between them, she thought of how important he was becoming to her.

"I'd better get home. I've got a lot of arrangements to make. I'll—"

"I'll stay with your children while you're gone. They can either come out here or I will stay with them at your place." He took her hands. "The important thing is that you don't need to worry about them. Go be with Cara. Help her through this."

Stunned by the offer, she couldn't think of a thing to say.

"Sarah will be around to help, too, but since the twins are a handful, I thought—"

She put her fingers against his lips to still his words. "I accept. I need to be there for Cara, and if you don't mind me being gone for four or five days, I can't think of a better solution. Sean already spends a lot of time out here, and my other kids love the ranch. Thanks for offering."

"Friends help friends. That's what I've been trying to tell you."

She gathered up her purse to leave. Friends, yes that was all they were. But she couldn't help the disappointment that seeped into her heart. When had she started wanting it to be so much more?

Chapter Ten

Sweat poured off Peter's face as he guided the wheelbarrow full of plants into the interior courtyard at the second home being built by the *More Than Dreams* show. After emptying his load, he surveyed the progress. With the house enclosing the large area on all four sides, this space would be a safe place for the children to play. The show's designers knew what kids liked.

"I can't wait to see it completed and furnished tomorrow." Laura handed him a tall paper cup of ice water.

He drained the liquid, relishing its coldness as it slid down his parched throat. "I still can't believe this is happening. They move fast when they make up their minds. Just weeks ago this was a dream."

"Hence the title of the show. I imagine others have felt the same way." Laura snatched the paper cup from his hand. "Want any more?"

"Nope. That hit the spot. August seems to be unusually beastly this year."

"I heard there's a cold front coming in tonight with

a chance for rain. Tomorrow's only supposed to be in the mid-nineties."

"What will we do with all that cool weather?"

"And don't forget the rain."

Laura's laughter penetrated his heart with warmth. He was glad she was laughing. The past few weeks since she returned from the funeral in St. Louis she had been quiet, withdrawn. "What's rain? I've forgotten what it is. Refresh my memory."

"You know water that comes down from the skies." Laura crushed the paper cup in her hand. "If it does rain, we'll have more than the completion of the houses to celebrate at the party tomorrow night."

"*If* is the operative word." As much as he loved talking with Laura, the sounds of hammers and saws coming from inside the cottage called him back to work. Peter picked up the handles of the wheelbarrow and started toward the sliding-glass doors that led into the large family room. "Besides delivering water, what have you been doing?"

Laura walked alongside him through the house and out onto the porch that ran the length of the front. "Helping put the kitchen together." She waved her hand down the length of her. "Can't you tell?" She pointed to a bright cobalt-blue blob on her denim shorts. "This is the trim and this—" she touched a yellow streak on her T-shirt "—is an accent color."

"I see you're still messy with a paintbrush."

She flashed him a saucy smile. "Well, my break is over. Back to work. We only have twenty-four hours to the big wrap-up party."

While Laura went back inside, Peter paused on the porch. Hundreds of volunteers were scrambling to finish the two houses. Some were people from school. Others were friends from church. But there were a lot of strangers who had offered a helping hand.

"Peter, do you want anything to drink?" Sadie stopped beside him with a tray full of cups of water.

"Laura just brought me one." He'd seen Sadie earlier at school. Although the students didn't start until next Tuesday, the day after Labor Day, he and the staff had been dividing their time between working at the school and here. The fact that the whole high school staff had volunteered to help shouldn't have really surprised him. The people he worked with were generous to the point where many were putting in long hours at both places.

"I'm gonna have to have a word with her about taking my job. This is about all I can do." She glanced down at her rounded stomach. "It won't be long. Actually should have already happened. Andrew is beside himself. He should be here somewhere. He's so excited about becoming a father again. This time he's sure it's a girl."

The mention of Andrew being excited, coupled with Sadie being very pregnant, brought back memories of three years ago when Diana announced to him that she was going to have a baby—another man's. The betrayal he experienced at the moment still stunned him even today. She'd had an affair with a neighbor, gotten pregnant and was leaving him to marry the man. She'd relished telling him that her lover had been able to give her what he couldn't—a baby.

"Peter, are you okay?"

He heard Sadie's words as though she were yards away from him instead of inches. He curled his hands so tightly that pain shot up his arms. "I—I'm okay." He tried to smile, but the corners of his mouth quivered.

"Has the heat gotten to you? Here, take another drink." With concern etched into her features, Sadie thrust the whole tray toward him.

"No, I'm fine really. I just remembered something."

A doubtful look pinched her lips into a frown. "You want me to go get Laura?"

"No!" He said it so fast even he was surprised.

Laura was the last person he wanted to see while his emotions raged and waffled. Diana's infidelity underscored all the reasons he needed to be cautious in any relationship with another woman. Diana had taken his heart and stomped all over it. The few times he'd seen her since the divorce had wrenched him with thoughts of what could have been. The more attracted he became to Laura the more he thought about his ex-wife. How could he put his heart on the line when he hadn't forgiven Diana? That realization struck him like a wrecking ball knocking down an old abandoned building.

"Maybe I will take another cup of water." Peter snatched one from the tray and downed it. "I'd better get back to work. There's still a lot that needs to be done."

"Okay, boss," he heard Sadie say as he hurried away with his wheelbarrow to get more plants.

Why hadn't he realized he hadn't forgiven Diana?

Why had he thought he'd worked his way past the hurt? *Probably because I haven't dwelled on what happened in the past. In fact, I've made it a point not to think about what transpired those last few months with her. But there's no way I can go forward with Laura, feeling this way. It wouldn't be fair to her.*

He'd known Laura had been running away from her past but to discover he had, too, still stunned him fifteen minutes later when Jacob cornered him in the courtyard.

"Peter, slow down. We're going to get this done in time for the party."

Peter paused in lifting the last bag of mulch from the wheelbarrow. "We still have so much to do."

"Are you planning to stay late again?"

Peter dropped the bag onto the cement near the flower bed. "Yes. I'm not sure we can complete the houses in time." He starting pouring the mulch around the begonias.

Jacob gripped his arm. "Want to talk about what's really bothering you?"

"What do you mean?"

"I know you, Peter. We've been friends for years. I think of you as a brother. You're upset. It's written all over your face. Is it Laura? I saw you talking with her earlier."

Peter frowned. "It's Diana."

"Oh."

There was a wealth of meaning in that one word. Jacob had been there for him through the divorce. He'd seen Diana's baby at the hospital hours after he had been born. Jacob had been the one who'd made him realize he had to go on with his life. "For the past few years I thought I was over what had happened to Diana and me. Yes, I was cautious about getting involved, but I attributed that to being gun-shy. Today I found out that wasn't really the case."

Jacob pulled him away from the others working on the courtyard. "You aren't over Diana? You still love her?"

Peter shook his head. "It's not that. But when I was talking with Sadie, all of a sudden I realized I'd never forgiven Diana for getting pregnant with another man's child."

Jacob's brow creased. "But you've been around Sadie for months. You two work together. She's involved in the fund-raiser."

"I know. But when she began talking about how excited Andrew was about becoming a father again, something clicked in my brain. I'm still carrying around a lot of anger. Anger I thought I dealt with."

Jacob cocked his head to the side. "Does Laura have anything to do with this new revelation? I know how much you care about her. Does that scare you? Are you using Diana as an excuse to back off?"

"You are just full of questions."

"And you're avoiding answering me."

Peter wanted to avoid his friend's inquiries, but Jacob wouldn't let him. He knew him too well. "How can I move on when I feel such anger at Diana for betraying our vows? Will that happen again? I don't want to be alone. I want children running all over the place. Is that why I'm attracted to Laura? She has four kids who are wonderful. That was only confirmed when I took care of them while she was in St. Louis." Peter raked his fingers through his sweat-drenched hair. "If I ever marry again, it has to be forever. I can't go through what I did with Diana again."

"Are you sure it isn't cold feet the closer you get to Laura? I've seen you two together and there are definitely sparks flying. I'm envious. I want that one day."

"I need to be one hundred percent sure. I don't ever want to hurt Laura or her kids."

"Of course. But you know nothing is a guarantee except the Lord's love. We make the best choices we can and hope for the best."

Tension seized Peter's neck muscles in a tight hold. He kneaded his fist into his nape. "After what happened with Diana, I can't have a relationship with secrets. And Laura is keeping some. She won't let me in."

"Have you been totally open with her, especially about Diana?"

Jacob's question plagued him far into the night. Even when he finally laid his head on his pillow, he couldn't sleep. He hadn't let Laura in completely, either. There was always a part of him he held back. What a pair they made. As he had begun to get to know Laura, he'd actually started to think he was ready to date, to get involved with a woman, to marry again. Now he knew better.

The festive air of the *More Than Dreams* final taping stirred Laura out of her exhaustion. The balloons, the signs, the food, the volunteers were all in place. She stood at the front of the crowd, waiting for Peter, Noah,

Jacob and Alice to arrive to do a walk-through of both houses with the show's host.

Someone jostled Alexa, and she bumped into Laura. "Mom, look at all the people. I'm glad we got here early."

After finishing up the kitchen, Laura had gone home a few hours ago to dress for the taping and party. As one of the board members of the foundation, she knew she would be in the front of the mass of people because of their involvement.

"Look, there's Alice." Joshua pointed toward the silver Lexus that pulled up in front of the cottages. "She's using a cane. Is something wrong with her?"

"It's been a long week. That's all," answered Aunt Sarah, who stood on the other side of Laura.

Was that all? Laura wondered. She studied Alice's slow gait. Laura realized that the past week had been hectic even for Alice who hadn't done any of the physical labor. But she had been interviewed more than once and had been in the middle of all the chaos. She loved every minute of it, but the tired lines had deepened as the week progressed. Alice probably wouldn't admit it, but being on this show was one of her dreams coming true.

What is my dream?

She would have said when she'd first come to Cimarron City to get her own place, to provide for her family and pay off her debts. Now she didn't know. When she thought about Peter, confusion reigned. There wasn't one indication he was anything like Stephen, and yet fear and guilt kept her from taking the next step with him.

Maybe her dream should be to know what her dream was.

She laughed at the thought.

"What's so funny?" Sean said, having pushed his way closer to her.

"Oh, nothing. Where have you been?"

"Taking care of the animals in the barn. Chad helped. I told Peter I would, since I knew he wouldn't be able to."

What if she continued to see Peter? How would Sean take it? They hadn't talked much, both of them being so busy with the foundation and the Shepherd Project. Although her eldest spent a lot of time at the ranch, especially since it was summer, there was still a reserve between Peter and her son, as though Sean wanted more but wasn't sure about it. Much like her. She needed to have that conversation with her teen. She couldn't disrupt her children's lives any more than she already had, especially Sean's.

"They're going inside." Matthew tugged on the sleeve of her soft peach-colored dress, the only thing she had bought for herself in a long time.

The group entered the first house with the camera crew filming it all. She'd have to wait until the program aired to see Peter's reactions to a few of the surprises she knew had been brought in after he went back to his house to get ready and to pick up Alice. Computers for the kids. A van in the garage. A state-of-the-art office for the house parent. A whole array of games in the family room.

"When do we get to go through?" Alexa asked.

"As soon as the group moves to the other house, we can have the grand tour."

"Really?" Joshua hopped from one foot to the other. "Before everyone else?"

"Yep, kiddo. Mom's on the board." Sean slapped him playfully on the top of his head.

Ten minutes later Laura with her family and the others who were involved with her in the fund-raiser were allowed to go into the first cottage. The producer wanted their reactions taped for the show, as well. She wondered how it all would be spliced together.

Laura linked her arm through Aunt Sarah's and headed up the steps. Although she'd seen most of the house, awe still washed over her as Laura went through it—enough bedrooms and baths for eight foster children and one house parent or couple, a large family room and dining room with a long table that seated twelve, a well-equipped kitchen and a laundry room with two washers and dryers. Beige tiles covered the floors in all the common rooms while a medium brown carpet was in the bedrooms. Large windows brought the outside into the cottage, making the place cheerful, warm. And all this had been built in a short time because of the tons of people involved in the construction. Amazing!

"Mrs. Williams, you're one of the board members of the Henderson Foundation. How do you feel today about seeing the completion of the houses?" a production assistant asked while a cameraman filmed her response. Another person from the local television station was present, too.

"Elated at this beautiful job the *More Than Dreams*

team did here. The cause is such a worthy one. Many foster care children will benefit from this."

"Are you accepting donations?"

"Yes. We'll be having our first fund-raiser the second Saturday in September at the Cimarron Hotel downtown. It's a dinner and auction with such items as a trip to Disney World, the use of a leased car for a year, a new computer and printer. The proceeds will go to running these two homes. We hope to have them open by the end of September." She knew that the local reporter would be using part of her interview to publicize the auction and the upcoming *More Than Dreams* show.

After she spoke to the production assistant and he, the cameraman and local reporter moved on, Alexa grabbed Laura's arm. "Mom, you'll be on national television."

"If I am then so are you because you were right next to me." She'd been interviewed on several occasions, and it was still hard for her to believe she would be on TV for millions to see.

Her daughter's eyes grew round. "That's right."

Laura laughed as the realization took hold of Alexa. She straightened, her shoulders thrust back, a huge grin on her face. A lump jammed Laura's throat at the sight of her happy children. Joshua and Matthew were exploring the large family room, looking through some of the games stocked in the cabinet while Sean had disappeared outside to the courtyard.

Thirty minutes later Laura and her children had viewed both cottages and made their way toward the backyard where a tent was set up for the celebration.

Although most of the filming was finished, there was one camera crew weaving their way among the guests taking candid shots of the festivities.

"How are you holding up?" Peter said from behind her.

She pivoted, surprised she hadn't heard him approaching, but then she shouldn't be because the noise level was high, forcing her to answer him in a loud voice. "By sheer willpower. Now that the excitement is winding down, so am I."

"I think that's how Alice feels. Jacob took her home."

"She's gone?" Laura scanned the crowd.

"Yes, five minutes ago."

Strange. She would have expected Alice to say goodbye. But then nothing was normal since the production crew had come to Cimarron City a week before. She'd pay Alice a visit tomorrow and see how she was doing. "How are you holding up?"

"Personally, I'm thinking this is what shell shock is like. Numb. Not sure if I can string two words together coherently, especially on camera. I guess we'll find out in four weeks when the show comes on and the whole world sees."

"Is that panic I hear in your voice?"

"More like terror. I just hope I represented the Henderson Foundation well."

Laura touched his arm. "You did great. Besides, you're the Henderson Foundation. This wouldn't be happening if it weren't for you."

He took her hand. "C'mon. Let's find someplace where we can actually carry on a conversation without shouting."

He went into one of the cottages through the kitchen and didn't stop until he was standing in the courtyard. A few lights streamed through the windows, crisscrossing the cement while the moon's rays bathed them in a soft glow from above. Peter tugged Laura close.

He sighed. "Ah, the sound of semi silence. Wonderful. Much better."

"It will be nice to get back to a normal routine."

"With school starting on Tuesday and the fund-raiser the following Saturday?"

"Yeah, what were we thinking?"

"About the kids. The faster we can get everything in place the faster they will have a home." His expression sobered.

"I knew there was a reason I'm working 24-7. Well, not exactly 24-7, but it sure feels like it," Laura said with a laugh, wanting to interject some humor into the suddenly somber atmosphere.

Peter stepped back. "This is the first opportunity I've had to talk to you in private in say a week. I have something I'd like to tell you."

His serious tone made what little strength she had drain away. She crossed to the wooden bench and sat, the sound of the fountain behind her soothing and almost drowning out the distant noise from the party and her thundering heartbeat. Peter remained standing a few feet in front of her, the shadowy light hiding his features.

"I've told you about my ex-wife and our divorce, but I left something important out. She was pregnant with another man's baby when we divorced. I'd known she'd wanted her own child, but I hadn't realized the extent of that desire." He paused, his chest rising as he drew in a deep breath, then falling as he released it slowly. "When she told me about being pregnant, her betrayal nearly crushed me. Before I realized I couldn't have children, I'd dreamed of her carrying my child. Then there she was before me carrying another man's."

The pain in his voice pierced through her heart. She came to her feet and covered the space between them in two long strides. "I'm so sorry, Peter. I'm—there are no words to say to make it better."

"I thought I was fine until lately. What I've finally realized is that I've never forgiven Diana for what she did. I've harbored this anger deep inside. Every time it started to surface, I squelched it subconsciously."

"What's changed?"

"You in my life."

His answer stunned her. "Me? I don't understand."

"I've started to think of us as a couple. I want there to be more between us, but I haven't resolved some of my issues concerning Diana. I have to find a way to forgive her."

"Why?" Laura thought of her own feelings toward Stephen. Forgive him? She didn't think she ever could.

"Because these feelings are poisoning me. She's already harmed me. I need to put an end to it."

"You make it sound so simple." It wasn't for her, not where Stephen was involved.

Peter shook his head. "It isn't. If it was, I would have done it three years ago. But I do know I can't do it alone."

"What are you going to do?"

"Pray for an answer." He clasped both of her hands and drew her up against him. "I want to move on. I don't want bitterness and anger from my past to affect my future anymore."

Neither did she, but she didn't have the confidence he did that it wouldn't. Would praying help? She still felt she was fumbling around with her attempts at prayer.

Peter shifted and the rays from the moon, coupled with the lights from the house, accentuated his face, a smile softening his expression. His arms encircled her.

"You are my inspiration to get on with my life. As I was touring the houses with the camera crew following me and recording my every move, all I could think about was you and how much has changed since I've gotten to know you. I've gotten the Shepherd Project up and running and started the Henderson Foundation. I'm doing something I've wanted to do for a long time, and I have you to thank for that."

His words swelled her heart. Stephen would never have said something like that to her. Memories of his hateful comments threatened to destroy the mood between her and Peter. *I won't let them!* She shoved them back in the box, slammed the lid and ignored their taunting shouts. She snuggled against Peter.

He laced one hand through her hair, cupping the back of her head, while he lowered his mouth over hers. The touch of his lips on hers spoke clearly of his intentions to include her in his life.

"Mom! Aunt Sarah—"

Laura wrenched away from Peter, swinging around to face Sean, who had come out into the courtyard.

Her son glared at both of them, his hands opening and closing at his sides. Suddenly he whirled on his heel and rushed back into the house. A few seconds later the sound of the door slamming shut echoed through the house.

She'd just gotten her answer about how Sean really felt about Peter and her. "I'd better find him and talk with him."

"Laura, let me first. Man to man."

"No, I can't!"

"Why not? He needs to know my intentions are honorable."

"No, you can't say anything to him," she yelled, surprised by her raised voice. With Stephen she'd never raised it because he would always hike his level up even more. "This is between me and Sean," she added, still several decibels louder than normal.

"In other words, I shouldn't be concerned with a family matter."

His tone was even, a thread of steel and something else—hurt?—in it but not seething anger that manifested itself in screaming. "Our relationship has improved over the summer. I can't risk it going back to him stomping around the house, angry and silent with me. Sorry." Laura hurried after her son, aware that Peter remained in the courtyard. Aware she had hurt him.

Chapter Eleven

Fifteen minutes later Laura found Sean holding his lamb in the barn, sitting on the ground, leaning back against a stall door. He stared at a spot before him and didn't look up when she came in.

She approached slowly and sat next to her son. *Give me the wisdom to reach my son, Lord.*

"Hon, you know I've been seeing Peter."

He twisted toward her, his eyes pinpoints. "I thought you were working together on the fund-raiser. I thought—" he sucked in a gulp of air "—never mind what I thought. It isn't important."

She laid her hand on his arm. "Yes, it is. Lately it seemed like you two were getting along. You didn't mind staying with him while I was in St. Louis."

He shrugged away from her touch. "He's okay, I guess. It's just…" He clamped his mouth closed on the rest of his sentence.

"What, Sean?"

"I don't want you to get married again, not after—" he swallowed hard "—after Dad."

He doesn't want anyone to replace his father in my life. Tears smarted her eyes. *It's only been fifteen months since Stephen's death. Maybe in time Sean will change his mind. Until then how can I deny my son's request when he's hurting so badly?* Her son's pain became hers. "Honey, I'm not getting married again. Peter and I are good friends. We've been thrown together a lot because of the foundation, but we aren't anywhere close to discussing marriage."

"You aren't? He was kissing you."

His accusation blasted her in the face. "We shared a kiss. That's all." No, it wasn't. It was much more than that. It was…she didn't have an answer. Laura wanted to scream her own frustration at her spiraling emotions spinning out of control where Peter was concerned. She didn't want to fall in love. It complicated everything!

"I know what Joshua, Matthew and Alexa have been doing. They're trying to get you two together. I told them to stop it."

So that was why nothing had happened in the last month, Laura thought.

"Are you sure there's nothing to worry about?" His gaze reflected his concern.

No, I'm not sure. But I won't lie to Sean. "We haven't discussed marriage."

"Good." Relief smoothed the creases on his brow. "Did I tell you I get to use Louise here as my project for the FFA this year?"

"No. That's great, but where in the world did you come up with a name like Louise for a sheep?"

"It stands for St. Louis."

"I see." He'd hated moving here, but she had thought as his friendship with Chad had grown that he was adjusting. Now she wasn't so sure about that. "Maybe during fall break in October we can take a few days and go to St. Louis, visit your dad's grave, see some old friends. It will be good to check on Cara."

"Yeah, I guess," her son mumbled, suddenly closing himself off from her. He shoved to his feet. "I need to put Louise back with Bessie." He walked outside toward the pasture where the sheep were.

One step forward, two steps back. Laura shook her head, not sure how successful their talk had been.

The next morning Laura rang Alice's doorbell and waited. A few minutes later she did it again, but still nothing. Maybe Alice wasn't home. Pressing her ear to the wood, Laura listened. Sounds of the TV floated to her. Alice told her last night that she would be glad to get back to her routine and see her television shows she'd missed these past few weeks with all the preparations for the taping. Then why wasn't she answering the door?

She dug into her purse and withdrew her cell phone. She punched in Alice's number, and when she didn't answer, she called Peter.

"Do you think Alice went somewhere and left her TV on?" she asked when he answered.

"No, never. She's a stickler about making sure it's off when she's not watching. It wastes money otherwise. Why do you want to know?"

"I hear the TV, but she's not coming to the door. I'm worried."

"I have a key. I'll be there in ten minutes. I'm at school. See if the manager is home and will let you in."

When Laura hung up, she scanned the foyer and saw the apartment with a gold plaque on its door that read Manager. After hurrying across the hall, she kept her finger pressed on the bell. A good minute later, she gave up, went back to Alice's apartment and pounded on her door.

Shortly, Peter rushed into the building, taking a key out of his pocket. His hand shook as he stuck it into the lock and turned it, his face carved in grave lines.

Inside the blare of the television chilled Laura. She entered the living room right behind Peter and immediately saw Alice slumped on the floor next to her favorite lounge chair in front of the TV. Laura switched the set off while Peter felt for a pulse and checked Alice's breathing.

Please, Lord, let her be okay.

"She's alive." Peter flipped open his cell phone and called 911.

"Has she ever lost consciousness before?" Fear roughened her voice.

"No, but she's been pushing herself lately, not taking care of herself. I should have seen the signs and done something. I should have made her come live with me."

Peter twisted toward Laura and the expression of pain on his face threatened her fragile composure. Losing it would do no one any good. Peter and Alice needed her. "You can't make anyone live with you if they don't want to."

"So you've told me." His voice held an accusation.

Did he blame her for this? Laura drew up rigidly tall. "I'm not the cause, Peter. When we talked, I told you my opinion on how Alice would feel if you tried to force the issue of her moving in with you."

He blew out a long breath. "I know. I shouldn't have listened."

She wasn't hurt by his words. She wouldn't let herself be. Apprehension ruled Peter right now.

The shrieking sound of the siren grew nearer and came to a stop. Laura hurried toward the door. "I'll bring them in here."

Out in the foyer the emergency crew brought in a gurney. Inside the apartment Laura stood back with Peter next to her watching the EMTs prepare Alice for transporting to the hospital. Despite his words earlier, Laura slipped her hand around Peter's. He needed a friend. The feel of his cold skin against her highlighted the seriousness of the situation.

Five minutes later after Alice was loaded into the ambulance, Laura faced Peter. "You're coming with me. I'm driving." Her voice defied him to argue with her.

He nodded his head once and followed her to her Ford Escort. The fact he didn't insist on driving himself spoke more than words about how worried and distressed he was.

Laura gripped the steering wheel to keep her hands from trembling as she drove toward the hospital. "She will be okay. We got to her in time," she said to break the strained silence.

"We don't know that for sure. She saved my life

when she and Paul took me in. I couldn't do anything about Paul dying, but I'm going to do my best not to let Alice die."

"Peter, if it's her time, there's nothing we can do. It's in God's hands."

He twisted toward her, his expression fierce. "Do you really believe that?"

She thought for a moment and realized she did really mean it. When had she come back home to the Lord? Going to church, reading her Bible again had played a part in her homecoming, but mostly it had been Peter and his quiet way of persuading. "Yes, I do. If I've learned anything from Mason's untimely death, I've learned that."

Did that mean that Stephen's death had been in the Lord's hands, not hers?

The unanswered question settled in her mind as she searched for a parking space at the hospital. It stayed with her as she and Peter rushed into the emergency room, only to be directed to the waiting room while the doctor and nurses worked on Alice.

She sat in a chair, glad the room was vacant at the moment. Peter paced from one end to the other. Her thoughts churned with that brief conversation in the car. She wanted to let go of her guilt over Stephen so badly. But it had been so much a part of her life for over a year that she didn't know if she could. It sounded so simple. It couldn't be that simple. Nothing had been simple for a long time.

"Do you want some coffee?" She couldn't stay there and watch Peter pace any longer. She needed to do something herself.

"No." The stress in his voice underscored the deep lines in his face, the ashen cast to his skin.

She went down the hall to the vending machine and put her money in it. When she took her cup out of the slot, her hand trembled so much some of the hot liquid sloshed over the rim onto the floor. She placed the coffee on a ledge nearby, then laced her fingers together.

Lord, watch over Alice and help Peter to deal with this. Something has been triggered in Peter that goes beyond Alice's illness. I just feel it. Please guide me in how to be there for him.

When her hands felt steady enough, she took the cup from the ledge and headed back to the waiting room. Knowing God watched over them gave her the strength to return to Peter. Although his back was to her, his gaze swept to her immediately when she appeared in the entrance.

Disappointment marked his features. "I thought you were the doctor. What's taking them so long?"

"They'll get back with us when they have something to tell us. Have you called Noah and Jacob?"

"Yeah, while you were gone. They're coming after they call some more of her foster children."

"C'mon. Sit while you have a chance. It might be a long day." She urged him toward a chair then took the one next to him.

"Alice wasn't taking care of herself."

"There has been a lot going on lately."

"She wasn't even before the *More Than Dreams* show decided to build the houses. Remember that first time you met her? She didn't have much food in the kitchen.

She hasn't been eating properly and for a diabetic that is important. I tried but she would only let me do so much."

His anguish tugged at her. She covered his hand nearest hers. "She still thinks of you as one of her kids. She's the caregiver in her mind, not you."

"This wouldn't have happened if Paul had been alive. He could get her to do anything. If only I'd…" His voice faded into silence. He swallowed several times, averting his head.

"How did Paul die?"

Peter's shoulders slumped forward. "I let him down. If only I'd…" Again he couldn't complete his sentence.

His raspy words indicated she was on the right track. "That's the second time you said that. If only what?" she asked, determined to find out what was bothering him.

He turned toward her, a sheen to his eyes. "Paul had a heart attack while he was helping me in the barn. He loved to come to the ranch and see the animals. He liked to help clean out the pens and stalls. I couldn't stop him, just like I can't seem to get Alice to let me take care of her. When Paul fell over, I called 911 and had to sit there and watch him die because I didn't know CPR. I…" A tear slid down his cheek.

"It wasn't your fault."

"If I had known CPR, I might have been able…to save him. But—" he cleared his throat "—by the time the ambulance got there, he was dead."

"I'm gonna say this again. It wasn't your fault. It was his time. He's with the Lord now."

"But if I—"

She placed her fingers over his mouth and stilled his

words. "Don't beat yourself up over what-ifs. Did Alice ever say it was your fault? Did anyone?"

"No."

"Then why are you blaming yourself? Pray to the Lord. Ask for His peace. When something bad happens to someone we know and care about, we start questioning everything we've done. Could I have done this or that to change the outcome?" This time last year her anger at God would have prevented her from saying that to another. But as she had spoken the words, she'd meant every last one of them, as though the Lord had given her a script to read.

He shifted completely toward her and took her hands in his. "Laura, thanks for being there for Alice. If you hadn't been, no telling what would have happened. I hadn't planned on going to see her until this afternoon. Noah is in Oklahoma City and is coming back now. Jacob had an emergency at his office and is just finishing up with it."

"Alice is special to me. She reminds me of Aunt Sarah. I'll call her and the kids after we find out what's going on."

Keeping one hand linked with hers, he leaned back and stretched his legs out in front of him. "I'm glad you're here with me."

I'm glad I am, too. This is the only place I want to be. Here helping Peter. She refused to analyze her feelings at the moment. She could do that later when she knew that Alice would be all right.

When the doctor showed up, Jacob came in right behind him. Jacob joined Peter and Laura while the emergency room physician explained that Alice was stable and responsive now, but when she fell, she broke her left hip.

"What are her chances?" Peter asked the doctor, his voice thick and heavy.

"Good. She's a tough lady. As soon as her blood sugar is where it should be, she'll have surgery on her hip. We'll need to do a hip replacement."

"What kind of surgery will that involve?" Peter slipped his hand into Laura's.

"She should be up and walking in three days."

After the man left, Peter faced Jacob. "Will she be okay?"

"I think so. I won't kid you there are complications that can occur with a broken hip, especially at her age. But she will get excellent care here and recovery is so much faster now with a hip replacement. All we can do is pray."

Alice's pale, bleached look blended into the whiteness of the hospital's linens. Peter stared at her peaceful features and wished she were at his home, not here hooked up to a monitor and an IV drip. The constant beeping of the machine reassured him but at the same time grated on his frayed nerves.

Combing his fingers through his hair, he dropped his head and released a long breath. The past forty-two hours had taken their toll on him. The gritty feel in his eyes fought his desire to stay awake. Although Alice had come out of the anesthesia from her surgery and spoken to him, he needed to talk to her again when she was more coherent to make sure she would really be all right.

Peter massaged his neck, especially a knot under his ear that hurt when he moved his head to the left. Glad that Noah, Jacob and Laura had left a few hours ago, he inhaled the hospital scents that he was fast learning to hate. The sterile, antiseptic odor assailed his nostrils.

A rustling sound from the bed jerked his head up. Peter scooted forward in his chair and clasped Alice's hand. "Hey, sleepyhead. It's about time you woke up."

Scanning the private room, Alice blinked then focused on him. "Have you been here long?"

"How are you feeling?" he asked, not wanting to answer her question. She wouldn't be happy he had been sitting by her bed throughout the day and night—hadn't left the hospital since she'd arrived.

"Sore. Groggy. What happened?"

"Didn't they tell you yesterday in the emergency room?"

She scrunched her forehead, her eyelids half closing. "Everything is a little fuzzy. I remember I broke my hip." She glanced toward it. "I passed out at my apartment?"

"Yes. Your blood sugar went too low and you went into a diabetic coma. When you fell, you broke your hip, but the doctors say you can run in a marathon in a few months with your new hip."

She chuckled. "I think I'll pass. My marathon days are over." Licking her lips, she slid her gaze to the pitcher on the table beside the bed. "Can I have some water?"

Peter poured some into a plastic mauve-colored tumbler and stuck a straw into it. After adjusting her bed so she sat up halfway, he helped her take a drink.

When she was through, she looked at him. "So you're the one who drew guard duty."

"I volunteered. Gladly, I might add."

"Who found me?"

"Laura."

"Bless that girl. She's worth keeping around—" Alice directed the full force of her gaze at Peter "—if a man is smart."

"No matchmaking, young lady."

Her smile erased some of the pallor from her skin. "I haven't been young in ages. I think you need to ask Jacob for the name of a good eye doctor."

"My vision is fine. You're young where it counts, in your heart."

"Tell that to this old body." Her perceptive gaze assessed him. "Go home. You look like death warmed over."

"Thanks. That brings such a pretty picture to mind, especially in a hospital." The mention of death did bring to mind the conversation he'd had with Laura yesterday in the waiting room. "Did you ever blame me for Paul's death?"

Alice's eyes widened. "Why in the world would I do that? He had a heart attack."

"I couldn't do CPR. That might have saved him."

"Paul went to the Lord the way he wanted, quickly. He lived a good life and felt as though he'd served his purpose, so I would never have blamed you. You were with him when he died. He wasn't alone. I thank God for that."

These past few days seemed to be his time to

confront issues he'd suppressed. First Diana Friday night and now Paul's death. Laura was right. *People tend to overanalyze situations sometimes, especially when someone they love dies. What-ifs aren't the solution. They are the problem.*

"I'm gonna live so quit frowning, Peter."

"I'm sorry. I was thinking about something that happened the other day."

"Will you do me a favor?"

Peter leaned forward, resting his elbows on his thighs, his hands loosely clasped. "Anything."

"Let me help you. I haven't had much of a chance these past few years."

He knew exactly what she was referring to. When Diana left, he cut himself off from everyone, kept everything locked up inside of himself. If it hadn't been for Jacob cornering him one evening, he wouldn't have even known anything. Of course, it didn't take a rocket scientist to count back from when Diana had given birth to her son. "I discovered I hadn't really forgiven Diana for her betrayal. I said I had and I thought I had, but I hadn't. Even thinking about it right now pains me."

Alice frowned. "Do you still love her?"

"No. No. It's the thought of her sleeping with another man, and worse, giving him a child, something we had talked about, wanted for so long. How do I forgive her? She betrayed everything our marriage stood for."

She closed her eyes for a few seconds. "I haven't told another soul this, not even our minister. After Paul and I were going through a rocky patch in our marriage, early on, he had an affair. When I found out about it, I nearly left him. I would have except he begged me to forgive him. At first I couldn't. I tried. Then I turned to my Bible and read everything I could about forgiveness. By the time I finished, my anger was gone. I loved Paul. His affair didn't change that. I have never regretted forgiving him that day. The Lord knows what He says when He encourages us to let go of our anger and forgive those who trespass against us. Pray for the Lord's help." She yawned. "Son, I want you to go home and get some rest. You look awful. That way I won't feel guilty when I go to sleep."

He laughed and stood, kissing her on the cheek. "Leave it to you to tell me the unbridled truth."

"Always. That's why I want you to know I think that Laura would be perfect for you. Don't pussyfoot around and let her slip through your fingers."

Out in the hall he thought of what Alice had said about Laura. Obviously the subtle approach—if he could call what had transpired over the summer subtle—to matchmaking hadn't worked so Alice was going for a more direct one. He laughed again and made his way toward the chapel. He had some thanking to do and some thinking.

Laura entered the chapel, a simply decorated room with an altar and four rows of pews. The light through the large, round multicolored stained glass window danced across the maroon carpet in the front. She found Peter in the first pew.

When she'd seen his truck in the parking lot, she'd thought she would see him in Alice's room, but it had been empty except for Alice sleeping, a serenity about her. After checking in the cafeteria, Laura had decided to check the chapel. She strode to the front and sat next to him.

With his head bowed, he murmured, "Amen," then looked up, surprise fluttering across his expression. "I didn't expect to see you so soon. You should be home resting."

"When you have four kids, it can be hard to rest during the day. Is everything all right?"

"Better now that Alice is out of surgery and doing okay. The doctor says she'll be walking in no time."

"I saw her. She's asleep so I didn't want to disturb her."

"I need to head home. Feed the animals."

"Don't worry about that. I dropped Chad and Sean off and they're taking care of it. In fact, different members of the youth group will pitch in the next week so you don't have to do anything but be at school and make sure Alice is taken care of."

"Who organized that?"

"Me. The Shepherd Project is theirs now as much as yours. Let them do this for you."

His hand covered hers on the pew between them. "I'm amazed by your abilities. You just jump right in and take over. I haven't had to worry about a lot of things having to do with the foundation because of you. Thank you."

His compliment gave her the confidence to ask, "Then you won't mind doing a TV interview for our local station about the fund-raiser? It's getting near the time and I know we've gotten a lot of publicity with the show, but I want to hit this hard while we have that edge."

"When?"

"That's the bad part. They want to show it Wednesday so they will need to interview you tomorrow. I realize that's the first day of school so the timing isn't good for you. They want to get your reaction and comments on the aftermath of the *More Than Dream* show, then they want to do a follow-up after it's shown nationally."

He scrubbed his hands down his face. "I need a secretary or something."

"If the foundation grows as big as I think it will, how are you going to handle that and your job?"

His laugh held no humor. "I never thought about the heavy workload when I came up with the idea. In the past week we have received tons of donations so you're probably right."

"Haven't you discovered that I'm always right?"

"Actually I have."

Again Laura couldn't ignore the feelings his words generated in her. She felt as though she could handle anything. In all the years of her marriage to Stephen, she'd never experienced that. "Keep that up and my face will be flaming red."

"I like it when you blush."

He gave her a heart-melting smile that sent her pulse into overdrive. "Yeah, red is one of my favorite colors."

"One?"

"I have a lot of them. I never can choose just one. I love orange, yellow, red and pink."

"All the warm colors. That doesn't surprise me. Those are Alice's, too."

"I knew I liked her."

"I talked with her this morning about not being able to save Paul."

"And knowing Alice I'm sure she reassured you that it had been in God's hands, not yours when Paul died."

Peter cocked his head to the side, his eyes round. "You have gotten to know her well. That wasn't all I talked to her about. We discussed my inability to forgive Diana and she gave me some advice to think on. That was what I was doing in here."

"What advice?"

"To let go of my anger and to forgive. That anger only poisons us, keeps us from living our lives fully. It's like extra weight we carry around, dragging us down. I see that now. It caused me to pull back from life."

His words hit home. Laura felt exhausted from her emotions concerning Stephen, and yet it wasn't simply deciding not to be angry anymore, not when the pain had a stranglehold on her that went back years.

"Sitting here, I remember one important point. Jesus forgave the very people persecuting him on the cross. They were killing him and he forgave them! How can I do any less?" He took her hand again. "I know I can't do this alone. I need the Lord's help. Will you pray with me?"

She couldn't refuse his request. He'd done so much for her and her family. She bowed her head and opened her heart to Jesus, desperately needing to let go of her anger, too. To forgive, then forget.

Dear Heavenly Father, I'm trying but I can't get past it. I wish I was more like Peter and could forgive Stephen. How? Show me the way.

"Peter, what Alice told you could apply to me, too." The quaver in her voice italicized the shaky ground she was exploring. It wasn't easy for her to let someone into her life, and yet his words earlier about forgiving held a truth and wisdom in them she couldn't turn away from.

"How so?"

"I've told you that my marriage to Stephen was in trouble when he died. It was more than that. I spent years living with a man who put me down whenever he could. At the beginning it wasn't so bad, but the longer I stayed married to him the worse it got, especially as he lost more and more money gambling. I should have seen the signs before we got married, but I was so young and I thought I was in love with the high school football star. What a cliché. The cheerleader and the football star."

A memory invaded the peacefulness of the chapel. Two weeks before their marriage Stephen had found her writing in her journal. When she wouldn't share it with him, he had taken it and torn the pages into hundreds of pieces then thrown them at her. He'd stormed away as the paper fluttered to the floor around her. Two reasons had kept her from backing out of getting married: Stephen's wonderful, tender apology and the financial investment her parents had put into the wedding.

"Why did you stay?"

The tenderness in Peter's expression encouraged her to say more. "For my children. But even that isn't probably the total truth. I think I was afraid of the unknown. At least with Stephen I knew what to expect or at least I thought so until I discovered Stephen had gambled away our entire life savings and put us into debt. He'd lost his business and it wasn't going to be long before we lost our home."

The day the bank had called was the day her eyes had been opened fully about her husband. Finding out he hadn't paid the mortgage in four months floored her— still did even with the passage of time. But she had been clueless because Stephen had handled all the finances, would only give her a meager household allowance. She'd pinched pennies while he had been gambling away everything.

"I don't know if I can forgive him like you did with Diana. I want to, but it isn't that easy. There's so much…" Her throat constricted around the rest of the sentence, and she couldn't finish.

Facing her, he clasped her upper arms. "So much hurt?"

She nodded, unable to say anything. *Tell him the whole story.* She couldn't. It had been so hard giving him a glimpse into the emotional turmoil she'd lived in for years. She shouldn't have married Stephen, but when he had begun his mental games with her, she should have walked away from her marriage. Instead, she'd stayed. Now she realized her children had suffered, and they had been the very reason she had stayed.

He pulled her to him and held her tightly against him. The gentleness in his embrace nearly undid her. Peter was such a good man. But was she missing some subtle sign that he wasn't whom she thought he was? Could she trust her judgment now?

Peter pulled up to his house, exhausted from the past few days at the hospital and the emotional roller-coaster ride he'd gone through, but also at peace truly for the first time in years. Praying in the chapel with Laura had renewed his faith, and the fact that she'd finally opened up to him gave him hope there might be a future for them. When he had walked out of the place twenty minutes ago, he'd left behind his anger with Diana and had forgiven her for having an affair. He felt free and once he got some sleep, ready to take on the world—and his relationship with Laura.

When he started for his patio, he saw Chad head out into the back pasture, carrying a shovel. Peter took a detour toward the barn. He would check to make sure everything was all right with the animals then go get some sleep before he needed to be back at the hospital. His next goal was to convince Alice to come live with him—at least while she recuperated. Then once he got her to the ranch, hopefully she would see the wisdom in staying long term.

Entering the cooler interior, Peter scanned the well-maintained area, the scent of animals and hay permeating every corner. He realized more and more the kids were taking care of the pets, not him, since the foundation ate into his extra time. But what was so nice to see was Sean and Chad stepping up to take charge. The healing power of animals was working on Laura's son, and yet Peter felt something was bothering the teen. The anger, like Friday night, was still there waiting for a spark to ignite it. Why was he so angry? Was it his father's death or something more?

A sound from the last stall caught Peter's attention. He moved toward it. Inside Sean held a puppy, the runt of the litter, against his face, tears running down his cheeks and into its fur. For a moment Peter considered backing away and leaving the boy alone. Then Sean glanced up, saw him and scrambled to his feet, the animal still in his grasp, now against his chest. With his free hand he swiped his tears away.

"What are you doing here?"

The fury in Sean's voice battered at Peter. For an instance the exhaustion in him wanted to lash out at the teen. But his matching anger wouldn't solve the problem. He'd learned that from Paul. "I wanted to thank you and Chad for doing this." He kept his voice calm and steady even though Sean's face squinched into a scowl.

Laura's son pressed his lips together and glared at him. Both of the boy's hands now cradled the puppy against him as though the animal was a lifeline. And perhaps it was. Peter opened the gate and stepped into the stall.

"You've really taken a liking to this puppy."

Still Sean didn't say anything.

"How's Lady doing?"

"Fine."

"Maybe your mom will let you have another dog. This one could use a good home, too. I can talk to her about it if you want."

"Leave my mother alone!"

Whoa, this was worse than he had thought. Coupled with what had happened Friday night, Peter knew that Sean didn't want Laura to get involved in a relationship with him. Or was it more than that? A relationship with any man? After what Laura had revealed this morning in the chapel, he understood where Sean's feelings were coming from. Laura thought she had shielded her children from a lot of what Stephen had done, but he wondered how much Sean really knew was going on.

"Your mother told me what went on with her and your father."

"It's none of your business!" Sean's shouting scared the puppy who began to wiggle. He looked down at it and stroked it. "See what you made me do," he continued in a lower voice. He placed the animal on the ground and stormed toward the gate.

Peter followed Sean out into the center of the barn, a breeze blowing through the building and carrying an earthy smell. But its cooling effect did nothing to cool off Sean, who faced Peter, his hands fisted at his sides.

"My mom doesn't need a man. I'll take care of her and my brothers and sister, too."

The man of the house. He'd played that role for a while until his mother had died and left him completely alone. "What happens when you leave home after high school?"

"I'll—I'll…" He stared away from Peter, unclenching then clenching his hands.

"What's really going on here, Sean? What happened in St. Louis?"

"I don't want to talk about it."

"Maybe you should. Something is eating you up inside. Keeping it bottled up won't solve your problem. Believe me, lately I found that out for myself. I had to forgive someone who caused me a great deal of pain."

"I'll never forgive him. Never!" Sean shouted, a ferociousness on his face that reminded Peter of a rabid animal.

"Who?" Peter schooled his voice and expression into calmness as if he were taming a wild horse.

"Dad." The anger seemed to siphon from the teen as he collapsed onto a hay bale near him. He buried his face in his hands. His whole body quaked.

Peter kept his space, instinctively sensing the teen would bolt if he came any closer. "What did your father do?"

"He hit Mom, pushed her down the stairs. He hurt her, and I couldn't do anything to stop it. I should have been able to."

Sean's revelation knocked the breath from Peter. Laura had told him about the verbal abuse, but she hadn't said a thing about the physical. That realization hurt. She didn't trust him with her heart after all they had shared. "What happened?" he managed to ask, knowing he couldn't pass up this opportunity to help the boy even if he was shaking inside.

"They got into an argument. Mostly my dad yelled at Mom, said mean things to her, but this time she got angry back at him. I wanted to stop them, but I was afraid of what Dad would say. I was downstairs in the hallway. They were upstairs at the top of the landing. He yelled a lot those last months before he died. I just stood there and listened. They didn't know I was in the house. I'd come home early from a friend's." Sean lifted tear-saturated eyes to Peter. "The next thing I knew he'd slapped her and she'd fallen down the stairs. He ran out. I couldn't get to Mom in time to stop it. I think for a moment I just stood shocked that my dad would do that to Mom."

The picture that materialized in Peter's mind wrenched his heart. "What did she do when she saw you?"

"She was so upset I didn't say anything to her. She never knew I heard their fight. She thought I had just come in the back door, and I let her think that."

"How did she explain her fall?"

"She just said she'd stumbled, but she wouldn't have if he hadn't slapped her. I got Cara next door, and she drive Mom to the emergency room while I stayed with the twins and Alexa at Cara's. That evening instead of going home we went to a shelter." Sean sniffed and scrubbed at his face, wiping away his tears. "I know we went there because she didn't want him to find where we were staying."

"So you're angry with your father?"

"Yes!" Sean surged to his feet, the fury returning to make his body tense, his expression fierce. "I should have been able to protect her! Mom doesn't need a man to treat her like that."

"I agree. But not all men are like that."

Sean snorted. "I used to hear her cry herself to sleep

on the nights Dad was gone. For a long time I thought it was because she missed him. Now I know it was because she was relieved he wasn't around. Why did she stay with someone like that?"

That was the heart of the problem for Sean besides the feeling of helplessness he'd experienced when he couldn't protect his mother from getting hurt. "You need to talk to your mom and ask her that question. Don't keep this in here." Peter laid his hand over his heart. "You can't run from it. You have to face it and deal with it."

"Why should I now? I could have helped, but she never said anything to me."

Sean's last sentence confirmed whom Sean was really irate with. Yes, he was mad at his father, but Laura was the main target of that pent-up anger. "I imagine your mother was protecting you and your siblings. But you should talk to her. Your mother deserves that much. Give her a chance to explain her reasons for not saying anything."

"Sean. Peter, what's going on here?"

The sound of Laura's voice behind Peter brought forth his own anger, disappointment mingling with it. Why hadn't she told him everything this morning? Why did she continue to keep him at arm's length? What other secrets did she keep from him? he wondered as he pivoted toward Laura.

Chapter Twelve

Peter strode toward Laura, paused in front of her and said, "You two need to talk, then come up to the house."

"But won't you be asleep?"

"No," was his clipped reply, then he left the barn.

Laura watched Peter stride away, every line in his body transmitting anger. When she faced her son, he, too, conveyed how upset he was in the narrowing of his eyes, the tense set to his mouth and shoulders. There was nothing casual about his stance. He looked like a soldier, standing guard.

What did they talk about? Alarm skittered down her spine.

"What's happened?" she asked, covering the distance between her and her son.

"You told him about Dad!"

The accusation hit her with the force of a gale wind. "Yes." *Some of it but not all.*

"Why? It's none of his business."

"Because sometimes a person needs to talk to another about what they're feeling."

"You could have come to me."

One day Sean would understand some things were hard to discuss with a son or daughter. But right now, no matter what she said he wouldn't appreciate her reasons. "You can come to me, too."

"He knows about Dad hitting you."

Laura gasped. *He does?* "Hitting me? I didn't tell Peter that." *How do you know? What have you been keeping from me?* That was something she hadn't wanted anyone else to know except the counselor at the women's shelter, a stranger she had been able to walk away from. Not even Cara knew what really caused her to tumble down the stairs. Her alarm metamorphosed into panic that quickly spread throughout her.

Sean pulled himself up another inch. "I did. I told him that Dad slapped you and knocked you down the stairs."

"You knew about that? Why didn't you ever say anything?"

He lifted his chin as though to challenge her. "Why didn't you?"

Because somewhere in the back of her mind she hadn't wanted to admit that her son might have witnessed that humiliating scene between her and Stephen. She'd finally stood up to her husband and had ended up at the bottom of the stairs with thankfully only bruises and aches. "I didn't want you to think badly of your father. He was still your dad, no matter what happened between us."

"How often did he hit you?"

"That was the first time."

"I hate him!" Sean's voice thundered through the barn.

"That's why I never wanted you to know. I don't want you to hate your father."

"After what he did to you, why shouldn't I? He doesn't deserve my love."

"A wise man recently told me that if I can forgive someone who has harmed me, then I'm free, no longer bound by my anger. I don't want you to be held down because of your rage toward your father." As she spoke those words to her son, she saw the wisdom in letting go and finding the peace in forgiveness.

For if ye forgive men their trespasses, your Heavenly Father will also forgive you. She remembered the verse from Matthew and realized that in forgiving Stephen, maybe then the Lord would wash away her guilt at being responsible for her husband's death.

Sean paced a few feet away then spun around. "He tore our family apart. We had to leave our home. We stayed at a shelter, hiding from him."

"That was only temporary until I figured something out. For years your father was a good one who provided for you all. He'd gotten himself in way over his head and that had affected his thinking." At least toward his children. His opinion of her hadn't really changed, only worsened. "He loved you all. Don't ever doubt that, Sean."

Suddenly her son's rigid stance deflated, and his furious expression crumbled. "I killed him. If I hadn't argued with you about going to see Dad that night, he would still be alive."

"What do you mean? Your father drank half a bottle of whiskey and then took some pills. That's what killed him. That had nothing to do with you. It was his choice."

"You could have been there to stop him from killing himself if I hadn't gotten so mad."

How many times had she thought that very same thing never realizing Sean had, too? "I don't know if he committed suicide or not. But regardless of that, what happened was not your fault. You had nothing to do with it." *I did.* She strode to her son and drew him to her, praying he wouldn't reject her comfort because she needed to feel him in her arms.

"I couldn't protect you! He hit you! I never wanted to see him again. I didn't want you to."

The anguish-drenched words wrung her heart. She framed his face between her hands, forcing him to look at her. "It's my responsibility to protect my children. Listen to me. You are not to blame for a single thing. I'm beginning to discover how destructive blame can be. Don't blame yourself. Don't even blame your father. Let it go, honey."

The fight and anger emptied from Sean, and he sagged against her. Sobs racked his body and her heart. Nothing was worse than a mother seeing her child hurt so much. A child who had a difficult time letting her inside—too much like his mother. Her eyes stung with her own emotions clogging her throat. Wet tracks ran down her cheeks unchecked.

When his tears abated and his trembling eased, Laura quickly composed herself, then pulled back enough to look him in the face. "You did nothing wrong. You must believe me." If she did nothing else, she had to make him see that. She would protect herself and her children. Amazingly she was discovering she was strong enough to survive the hardships from a bad marriage.

"But I wanted to help you."

"You are, Sean. I've been so proud of you this summer taking on more of the responsibility of the project, working with the other kids and the animals." She cupped his face again, needing to make sure he understood. "I can't change the past. All I can do is move forward and learn from my past mistakes and believe me I have made some whoppers."

He blinked the last tear from his eye. A ghost of a smile graced his lips. "Not any bigger than some of mine."

"What a pair we make." Her laugh came out shaky but the tension in the air dissolved.

"Pair! I was supposed to help Chad in the pasture. Some animal is making holes, and we don't want the horses or sheep to hurt themselves. We're gonna fill them. I've gotta go. Are you coming back to get me or staying?"

"I need to see Peter. I'll be up at the house. How long do you think you'll be?"

"Thirty minutes, maybe a little longer. Chad's got half of them filled by now. He's probably not too happy with me right now."

"Just tell him I waylaid you and that I'll take you two to lunch. The pizza is on me."

With shovel in hand, Sean loped toward the back entrance. "That'll do it."

The second her son left, Laura sank onto a hay bale, her legs quivering. Sean had known all along about how bad it really had been that last day at the house with Stephen. She should have realized it. But when her son had appeared out of the blue after her tumble down the stairs, she'd been so distraught she hadn't been thinking straight. Then when he didn't say anything, she assumed he'd just come home and thanked God that he hadn't witnessed the fight. But he had and had kept quiet all these months, his rage festering inside him.

Thankfully Sean had never heard what Stephen had said to her on the phone when he had begged her to come back home that evening he had died. Her son was already dealing with enough. He didn't need to shoulder any more guilt. That seemed to be her job. But no more!

Laura pushed to her feet. *Because I want to put Stephen and my marriage behind me. I can't move forward until I do. I'm tired of that man still controlling my life. I'm taking charge. Now. Today.*

She strode from the barn and toward Peter's house. He deserved to know the whole story.

She knocked on his back door, and five seconds later, he opened it as though he had been waiting for her in the kitchen. On the table sat a cup of coffee, its aroma pervading the room.

When he saw her looking at it, he asked, "Do you want any? I just brewed it. I had to have something if I wanted to stay up."

"No." She moved farther into the room but didn't take a seat. "Why do you have to stay up? You should have come home and immediately gone to bed."

"We need to talk."

The dreaded words she'd known were coming dangled between them, taunting her resolve. For this she needed to sit down. After settling into a chair, she said, "I know that Sean told you about Stephen hitting me."

Peter paced to the pot on the stove and refreshed his coffee. "Why didn't you? I thought we had shared something today in the chapel. Funny how that illusion vanished when Sean started telling me about you falling down the stairs."

Sarcasm peppered each word, and she couldn't blame him for feeling that way. If their roles had been reversed, she would have felt as he did. "I'm sorry. I just couldn't. It isn't something I'm proud of."

He leaned into the table, his palms flat on its top. "You didn't do anything wrong with Stephen. He's the one who hit you."

"Don't you understand for years I was used to hiding his verbal treatment of me behind a cheerful front? I didn't want my kids to know. I didn't want my parents to know that my husband found me lacking in every way. I never could do anything right. That kind of behavior doesn't change overnight." Yes, she was beginning to see she had a lot to offer others and like Peter she wanted to spend her time helping children in need.

"But Sean knew."

"Yes, he did. I wish he didn't. He blames himself. Stephen caused so much damage and I let him. I don't know how I'll be able to forgive myself, let alone him."

"Until today I was sitting where you are. I don't ever want to go back to that way. Do what Alice did. Read the Bible on forgiveness and then search your heart. You need to forgive Stephen, not for him, but for yourself. Once you do, you can forgive yourself."

"After talking with Sean in the barn and pointing out to him how important it is that he forgive his father, I agree with you. I'm tired of holding this grudge against my husband. It takes too much energy I would rather spend somewhere else."

Surprise scored his features. "I was prepared to say more, but you took the wind out of my sails."

She stared at her clasped hands in her lap, feeling the drill of his gaze on her. "I have more to tell you. You might as well know the whole story and Sean doesn't even know all of it."

He sank into a chair across from her but didn't say anything.

"I'd been gone for a few days after the incident on the stairs. I took the kids and stayed at a women's shelter. I needed to decide what I wanted to do, and I didn't want Stephen to know where I was. I did know I couldn't go back to Stephen. Verbal abuse was one thing, but not physical. When he hit me, I finally figured out there was no way to save my marriage, that no matter what I did he would never be happy with me. It had been over a long time." She lifted her head and reestablished eye contact with Peter, afraid of what she would see in his gaze. She knew now the abuse hadn't been caused by something she had done, but for so many years she'd always wondered what she'd done wrong. If nothing else, Peter had shown her how a relationship between a man and a woman should be.

An unreadable expression greeted her inspection, actually giving her the courage to continue. "I needed to talk to Stephen to make arrangements to get our belongings when he wasn't there. I intended to take Cara and her husband with me so if he decided not to be gone I would have someone to intervene for me. But he wasn't there, so I had to leave a message for him to call me back on my cell. He did hours later, drunk."

A nerve in Peter's jaw twitched, his features hardening into an unyielding look. "What did he do, threaten you?"

"No, he was crying and begging me to give him another chance. He kept telling me he loved me over and over. I told him no, that I couldn't come back home."

"Good for you."

"It took me a while to get a backbone, but I was determined not to go back to him. The shelter had a wonderful support system in place. I knew if I went home he would hit me again and again until—" she shivered, hugging her arms to her chest "—until he put me in the hospital or the morgue."

His jaw took on the appearance of a piece of granite.

"But when I told him no, he began saying he would kill himself if I didn't come back to him. He had nothing else to live for." Tears glistened in her eyes. She didn't want to cry again. She'd shed so many in the past year and a half. "I decided to go see him. I guess I had thoughts of getting him some help. I just knew I couldn't let the father of my children hurt himself because I knew that when he was sober he wouldn't hurt himself. He was too selfish."

"Alcohol has that effect on people." Peter cradled his mug in his hands and brought it to his lips.

She noticed the slight tremor as he put it down on the table and peered at her, nothing revealed in his eyes although she'd heard sympathy in his voice. "Sean flew into a rage when I told him I had to leave to go see his dad. He pleaded with me not to go. Out of all my children I knew Sean was the most aware of Stephen's verbal attacks. I thought that's why my son didn't want me to go home. It took me fifteen minutes to get him calmed down enough that I felt I could leave. I went to my minister's house to get him. He was great at counseling, and Stephen needed it whether he would acknowledge it or not."

Thinking back to that night chilled her. She pushed to her feet and crossed to the coffeepot. After pouring herself a mug, she held the ceramic between her two hands, desperately seeking the heat emanating from the beverage. "When we got there forty minutes later, he was dead from mixing the alcohol with sleeping pills. There was a gun on the table nearby." So cold. She sipped at the hot liquid, but it did nothing to warm her. She took another drink. "I don't know if he intended to really kill himself, but if I had gotten there earlier, just left without saying anything to Sean, gone directly to the house instead of getting my minister, he might still be alive. I—I—" The tears spilled from her eyes and ran down her face.

Leaning back against the counter, with a shaky hand, she set the mug down before she dropped it. "Sean thinks he's responsible for his father dying. He isn't. I am." She remembered her words to her son about blame, but she'd been carrying it around for over a year, never sharing it with another until Peter. Old habits were hard to break.

Let it go.

I'm trying, Lord.

Peter shoved back his chair and was in front of her in two seconds. "No, you aren't!"

The force behind his declaration wiped the tears from her eyes. For a brief moment she thought about Stephen yelling at her that day on the stairs. Then she saw the compassion in the depth of Peter's gaze, always present, and knew there was no comparison between the two men.

"Don't you see? He's still doing a number on you. He was responsible for his own death. Not you. Not Sean. You did what you needed to do to protect your children, yourself. Have you ever thought about why he had the gun there?"

"To kill himself."

"Or you."

She'd been so wrapped up in feeling guilty for not making it in time to stop Stephen that she hadn't considered the gun being there to kill her. The thought rocked her foundation. Her legs weak, she clutched the counter to keep herself upright. "He wasn't a murderer."

"Anyone in the right circumstances might be driven to kill another."

She gnawed on her lower lip, trying to assimilate all that had happened in the past few days. All she had believed was ripped into shreds while her emotions lay floundering like a fish on a beach, not quite able to get back to the water.

Pain reflected in his eyes, Peter pivoted and started pacing. "Would you have ever told me the whole story if Sean hadn't said anything?"

"I don't know."

"Which says you don't truly trust me. I love you, Laura."

Stunned by his declaration of love, she couldn't think of anything to say for a few seconds. On the tip of her tongue were her own words of love, which surprised her as much as his.

He shook his head, though, and continued, "As much as it kills me to say it, I don't see how we can continue seeing each other if there isn't trust between us. My relationship with Diana lacked it, and I won't do that to myself again. I can't."

He was right. Would she have said something? Did she trust him completely? If she didn't, how could she really love him as he should be loved? She wasn't sure she had an answer for him—might never. When she had come inside a half hour ago, she had intended to tell him everything, then walk away from him. "Peter, I—"

The door slammed open, and Sean rushed into the kitchen. "There's a fire in the east pasture that runs along the highway. Chad and I tried to stop it from spreading, but it's out of control."

"Call 911," Peter said to Laura as he ran out of the house with her son jogging next to him.

She grabbed his phone on the desk and punched in the numbers. When the 911 operator came on, she said,

"There's a wildfire in the field along Highway 101, a mile out of town at Stone's Refuge."

"How big?"

"I don't know. I think it just started." Laura walked to the window over the sink to get a glimpse. Off in the distance black smoke rose into the air, sending dread skating down her spine. Not that far away, she thought. "I see a cloud of smoke maybe twenty feet across."

"I've alerted the fire department. There have been several wildfires in the area. You should get everyone to safety."

After hanging up, Laura hurried outside, the scent of smoke heavy in the air. The barn was in between the pasture and the house. She glanced over her shoulder at the two newly built cottages and released a sigh of relief. At least for now they were out of harm's way. But what if the fire couldn't be contained?

That question quickened her pace to a trot as she headed toward Peter and the boys. In the distance sirens blared their imminent arrival. A hundred yards away a line of flames ate across the meadow, slowly devouring its way toward the barn.

Peter assessed the rate and direction the fire was taking. "Let's move the animals to safety. Chad and Sean, empty the pens and stalls in the barn. What animals you can, put in my truck bed or in Laura's car. The bigger ones we'll have to hope can escape the blaze if they are freed."

Worry and fear sharpened Peter's voice. Letting the animals go wasn't easy for him. But they would have a better chance on their own than trapped in an enclosed area. "What do you want me to do?"

"Come with me. We need to drive the horses out of the pasture between the barn and the fire. I have a trailer we can put two of them in and hitch to the truck."

Which two would be his choice, and it would tear him apart to have to make that decision. She saw the distress in his expression as he realized what he would have to do if the fire spread. Worse, what would happen to his dream if the blaze consumed not only the barn and his house but the two cottages?

She hurried after him as the fire trucks raced down the gravel road toward them. *Lord, help us. We need Your help to fight the fire.*

Every muscle protested. Exhausted to the point of collapse, Peter paused and wiped the back of his hand across his forehead, sweat pouring off him. He peered toward the blaze still burning off to the east, but its spread had slowed down and the wind had calmed down some.

Lord, protect the animals. Protect the cottages.

Chad approached, carrying the lamb he took care of. "We've gotten most of the pets out. A couple I can't find. Bosco. The Great Dane. Molly."

"They're missing?" Laura swung the hose in an arc over the barn's side and roof, wetting down everything that she could, even the ground around the structure.

"We can't stay any longer. If the wind stays calm, hopefully the firefighters will be able to stop the fire before it reaches here. Either way we need to get to safety. Where's Sean?" Peter scanned the yard. The veil of smoke that hung over the ranch stung his eyes.

"I thought he was out here. He was gonna bring that puppy he loves to the car." Chad headed for the truck. "I'm riding in the back so I can take care of the animals until we get far enough away from the threat."

Dropping the hose, Laura shifted her attention to Peter. "What if Sean went looking for the missing pets? That's something my son would do."

"Keep spraying the water. I'll go look for him. Don't worry. I won't let anything happen to him."

Peter whirled around and went into the barn to make sure the teen wasn't anywhere inside. When he couldn't find any trace of Sean there, he hurried out the back entrance where his view of the blaze was unobstructed by trees. He estimated its distance was two or three hundred yards away. The firefighter's captain hadn't been too pleased he wasn't leaving the ranch right away. But there was no way he would abandon the animals he had come to love. He wasn't a fool. If it got too dangerous, he would, but he had to try to get them to safety while there was time.

He squinted when he thought he saw a person not dressed in a yellow firefighter's coat at the far end of the pasture nearest the barn. Sean? It was hard to tell with the haze that clung to the air. He took several steps forward, then a few more. It was Sean! The teen began to scale a tree.

Suddenly a burst of flames sprang up between Peter and Sean in the elm. "Laura," he shouted, backpedaling toward the barn. "Laura!"

"What's wrong?" She came around the side.

"Sean's in that tree. Probably Molly is, too." He

pointed toward the elm, the branches swaying more in the breeze. "Let the captain know about this new fire. I'll take care of Sean."

He rushed into the barn, grabbed a shovel then jogged toward the boy. His lungs burned as though the fire raged inside them. His head pounded with each step. Skirting the small blaze, Peter kept an eye on his surroundings in case another one popped up. A few feet from the fire a mound of dirt beckoned. He filled the shovel with it and headed back to the flames picking up momentum. After pouring the earth on the blaze, he repeated his actions until it was smothered out. Then he continued on his path toward Laura's son.

At the bottom of the elm, Peter searched the branches and found Sean reaching for Molly. "Get down. The wind's getting stronger. A fire was started in this field. I think I put it out, but we need to leave now." Peter glanced over his shoulder. Another fire sprang up near the old one, its yellow-orange flames striking alarm deep into his heart.

Sean looked through the foliage, his face paling when he saw the flames shooting up into the air so close. He snatched Molly from a limb and began his descent. "I heard her. I couldn't leave her up here by herself. She wouldn't come down."

"You heard her way out here?"

Sean leaped to the ground from the bottom branch, cradling the white cat against him. Averting his gaze, he mumbled, "Well, I went looking for her and that's when I saw her."

"Peter!"

He twisted around to see Laura coming toward him with a shovel in her hand. Halfway across the field another fire ignited right behind her, then another to her side. Fear as he'd never felt consumed him. Hot embers rained down on Laura.

Chapter Thirteen

I can't lose Laura. Peter raced toward her. Reaching her, he pounded the shovel into the ground, determined to stamp out the fire before the flames built to a raging inferno with the circle around her getting smaller and smaller until she had nowhere to go. Frantically looking around, he spotted some loose dirt and shoved his tool into the pile. He swung around and tossed it on one blaze while another sprung up next to it.

"Sean! Get some help," Peter shouted over the crackling of the fire.

His eyes watered, his throat was scratchy. The shovel felt as if it weighed a hundred pounds instead of ten. But he wouldn't stop until Laura was safe.

Through the dancing flames, Laura saw her son run toward the barn with Molly in his arms. Heat blasted Laura from all sides. She coughed from the smoke that had thickened into a black wall around her.

She wasn't going to let her children grow up without at least one parent. She attacked the ground with her shovel. Peter moved to do the same on the other side of the blaze. All she needed was a narrow path.

Lord, I need Your help.

As she watched the flames dancing around her, a calmness took hold of her. She would be all right. *Thank you, Lord.*

Suddenly Sean returned with the hose connected to the outside spigot on this side of the barn. He aimed the water at the fire closest to him, and it managed to shoot up in the air and fall only a few feet away. He yanked on the hose, trying to make it longer, but it was stretched as far as it would go.

"The captain is pulling some firefighters from the other field, but it may take a few minutes."

Over the hissing of the fire Laura heard her son's frantic voice as he explained. His jaw locked in determination while he continued to jerk on the hose.

Peter tossed his shovel down and ran toward the barn. Half a minute later, he disconnected the hose Sean held from the tap and screwed the one in his hands to the spigot. Soon the hose was long enough to reach the fire. Sean hastened forward, spraying the blaze around her.

Water pelted her, cooling her and the fire. An opening appeared, and Laura shot forward, escaping the blaze as firefighters came toward them. She raced toward the barn, flanked on either side by Peter and her son. When they reached the cooler interior, she fell into Peter's arms, her whole body quaking from exhaustion and relief. Sean neared her and Peter. She opened her arms to include him, relishing both of them pressed against her.

"Let's get out of here," Peter murmured against the top of her head.

"But what about the barn, your house?" She leaned away to look up into his handsome face. In that instant she knew she loved him with all her heart and she would fight for him.

"They are in God's hands. They can be replaced. You all—" Peter's gaze shifted between her and Sean "—can't be. I've got what I want right here."

"I'm sorry, Peter, Mom. I couldn't leave Molly up in the tree."

Peter clasped his hand on her son's shoulder. "I know. If I'd seen her, I would have done exactly what you did."

"You would?"

"Yep." Peter strode toward the front entrance, cradling them to him. "Let's get these animals to safety."

Tuesday, the first day of school, dawn broke across the eastern sky in bright pinks and oranges fingering their way through the blue, all traces of the black smoke gone. But its scent hovered in the air, along with the odor of charred wood and burned vegetation, as Laura climbed from her car parked behind Peter's truck. He'd returned home late the night before when the firefighters had decided it was safe for him. All the animals had been kept away, farmed out to friends until he could assess the damage and make sure they would be safe to come home.

At her house they had taken in Molly, Digger, the

litter of puppies and momma, Sean's lamb and two cages of rabbits. Her kids were busy caring for the pets until they could return to Stone's Refuge. She sneaked away to see Peter before they had to be at school, but not until she had talked with Sean to let him know where she was going.

Peter came out onto his patio with two mugs of coffee, obviously having seen her car approaching. He'd left her house only five hours ago, but during the hectic day before, they hadn't had any time alone and there was so much she needed to say to him.

She smiled and waved as she strode toward him. "You look ready to take on the world. Did you get any sleep last night?"

He shrugged, passing her a mug. "Maybe a couple of hours. If you find me asleep on my feet at work, wake me. I don't want the students to get the better of me the first day of school."

"You got a couple of hours more than me." She sat in a lounge chair and faced the yard.

In the distance the blackened field proclaimed the battle that had been waged the day before. She swung her gaze to the barn and sighed. The structure was intact, the blaze having come within twenty yards of it before the firefighters had managed to stop it.

"I made my rounds already, checking to make sure there aren't any hot spots left. So far, nothing. I'd feel a lot better if we'd have a good downpour."

"There's a fifty percent chance we will later today." She sipped her coffee, realizing both of them were skirting around the real reason she had come out here.

Lifting his drink to his lips, he caught her gaze over the rim. "So why didn't you get at least a few hours of sleep?"

"Every time I closed my eyes I relived being in the middle of the fire. I finally got out of bed, knelt by it and prayed. Yesterday could have turned out so bad, but it didn't. No animals died. No one was hurt. God is good."

"Amen."

"After I thanked Him, I opened my Bible and began reading the Word. By the time I put it down, I felt renewed, alive as I'd never been before." She scooted to the edge of her chair, leaning toward him. "I didn't get a chance to tell you how I feel about you. It's really very simple. I love you, Peter Stone."

He sucked in his breath.

"Yesterday you asked me if I would have told you the whole story. I know the answer today. Yes, I would have. It might not have been right away, but I've opened up to you more than I ever thought I would to any man after Stephen. When I was in the field with the fire surrounding me, I put my trust in the Lord, but I realized I put it in you, too." Her overflowing emotions crammed her throat from the awe and revelations the past twenty-four hours had brought her.

Peter clasped her hands in his. "I thought I was going to lose you yesterday. I wasn't going to let that happen."

"I came to Cimarron City to make a fresh start, to put the past behind me. What I forgot was that my past came with me. I wouldn't let it go. I couldn't forgive or forget. But over the months I've known you, you have been there for me every step of the way." She smiled. "I had never had that before so I resisted it, not sure if

I could trust it. I know better now. Stephen made his choice. I wasn't at fault for his death."

Rising, he squeezed her hands and yanked her into his embrace. "Yesterday when the wildfire started, I didn't think any good could come from it. I was wrong. I love you, Laura Williams."

He buried his fingers in her hair, holding her head still while he slanted his mouth over hers. As the seconds evolved into a full minute his kiss deepened, making it clear just exactly how he felt about her. She had never been cherished and the feeling elated her, making her tingle with awareness of the man in her arms.

"Before we talk about the future, I want to emphasize that I would have been attracted to you with or without your children. Yes, I want a family, but I would never marry a woman just for that." His mouth hiked up into a grin. "Besides, soon I'll have plenty of kids running around the ranch."

Laura barely heard what Peter said after the word marry. So eager to get on with the rest of her life, she raised one eyebrow and asked, "You want to marry me?"

He laughed, joy brightening his features. "I see no other way. I love you. You love me. I'm a logical kind of guy and the logic says we need to get married *soon*."

"I accept." She kissed him hard and quick. "And soon doesn't sound bad."

Seriousness leaked through his happiness. "We need to talk with your children. I want them to be okay about this. How do you think Sean will take the news?"

"Two days ago I would have said not well. Before I came this morning, I talked with Sean. I told him how I felt about you and that I hoped we could have a future as a family. He said fine then went back to caring for your animals in the backyard. I had planned to have a long discussion with him and that was all he said. When I didn't leave immediately, he glanced back at me, said that you know how to treat a woman right, then asked me what was keeping me from going to the ranch. I got the point and left."

"How about Alexa, Joshua and Matthew?"

"Are you kidding? You'll hear their cheers all the way out here when I tell them."

"Can we tell them together? I want to be there if they have any questions. Do you think they'll be okay with living out here at the ranch? Will you be okay with it?"

"I love your ranch, and Alexa will have her bags packed the second I tell her we're getting married. Horses and my daughter go hand in hand."

"Thank goodness all the horses were recovered last night."

"To give you credit, I think she would come if you didn't have any horses."

"Good." He snuggled close. "We're going to make two old ladies happy."

She chuckled. "It's gonna make their day."

Epilogue

"Mom, the show is almost on."

All the way into the kitchen Laura heard Alexa's shout from Peter's den. Laura hurriedly grabbed the bag of potato chips and made her way toward the room where her children, Aunt Sarah, Alice, Noah and Jacob were situated around a large television waiting for the *More Than Dreams* show to come on.

She put the potato chips on the coffee table next to the dip and other assorted food for this little celebration, then sat in the only available place left in the den, the ottoman to the chair where Peter was comfortably situated. Right where she wanted to be. Leaning back, she relished his arms around her, hugging her against him. Every day during the past weeks since Labor Day, she counted her blessings in having Peter in her life, in her children's lives.

"The next month is going to be busy. Are you ready for it?" Peter whispered into her ear, his breath tingling her skin beneath her ear.

"Let's see, there's the grand opening of the two cottages in a week and—" she tapped her finger against her chin "—I seem to have forgotten what else we need to do."

He nibbled on her ear, then murmured with a chuckle, "Nothing too important. Just a little wedding ceremony to go to and then the best part, the honeymoon."

"Oh, yeah. It must have slipped my mind." She shifted so she was face-to-face with him. "Why do we always plan everything important so close together?"

His love twinkled in his eyes. "Because your kids and I decided we didn't want to wait any longer than that and fall break is the third week in October. Besides, when you get back from your honeymoon, you're going to have your hands full managing the Henderson Foundation. You don't mind not working at the high school?"

"Not one bit. Managing the foundation is my dream come true."

"The donations have been pouring in, and after this show, I can't imagine them stopping. We've got plans to make."

She smiled, winding her arms around his neck. "A third house?"

"Then a fourth one. We've got the room." He kissed her lightly, then nipped at her lower lip.

"Hey, you two lovebirds, the show is starting. This will be your fifteen minutes of fame," Alice said, sitting near the TV set in her favorite lounge chair from her apartment.

Peter looked around the room. "We're going to have to add rooms to this house. Alice told me today she'll stay as long as I want her. Secretly, I think she's thrilled to be in the middle of all the kids. She loves children and yours are special to her. She once told me they make her feel young."

"That's wonderful. If Aunt Sarah ever decides not to live alone, we could build a little cottage out back for them."

"Shh, Mom." Sean took the remote and increased the volume.

"Peter, there you are!" Joshua yelled, waving his arm toward the television.

Laura settled back to watch the show, Peter's arms around her again, her head cushioned by his shoulder. She scanned the faces of her friends and family sharing this moment with her and Peter. Contentment flowed through her. She'd never felt more at home.

Thank You, Lord.

* * * * *

Look for Jacob's story,
HEART OF THE FAMILY,
out in December,
only from Margaret Daley and Love Inspired.

Dear Readers,

God knew what He was doing when He created animals. Of course, He always knows what He is doing. When I've had a particularly hard day, all I have to do is come home and hold my cat for a few minutes to feel better. The power of animals to heal is part of what this story is about. In *Once Upon a Family* Peter uses animals to help reach at-risk children, having been one himself. He rescues abandoned animals and uses them to rescue abandoned children. The other message in this book is about the critical need for quality foster care for children in need of a nurturing and loving place to live. Children are one of our greatest resources. We need to cherish and protect them.

I love to hear from readers. You can contact me at P. O. Box 2074, Tulsa, OK 74101, or visit my Web site at www.margaretdaley.com.

Have a blessed day,

Margaret Daley

QUESTIONS FOR DISCUSSION

1. Nowadays being a single parent is difficult. How did Laura deal with being a single parent? How could her faith have helped Laura raise her four children alone?

2. Laura felt the Lord had abandoned her because of what had happened in her marriage and after her husband's death. Instead of turning away from her faith, how could it have helped Laura if she had turned to God for comfort and guidance in her time of need?

3. In the end Peter felt that Laura didn't trust him enough to make a relationship with her work. How important is trust between two people in love? Is that different from two friends? How?

4. Laura endured verbal abuse for years in her marriage. When the verbal abuse turned physical, she finally got the courage to get out. How could her faith have helped her through the ordeal? Have you ever been verbally or physically abused? How did it make you feel? What did you do?

5. What is your favorite scene in the story? Why?

6. Forgiveness is important to our Lord. It is addressed in the Lord's Prayer. Laura and Peter both had to learn to forgive someone who had done something bad to them. Have you forgiven someone who did you harm lately? How do you feel about it? Do you feel free from your anger?

7. "Then said Jesus, 'Father, forgive them; for they know not what they do.' And they parted his raiment, and cast lots." This verse from Luke 23 is so powerful because it tells us how Christ forgave us as he hung on the cross, waiting death. What does this mean to you? How has this shaped your faith?

8. Peter is divorced because his wife betrayed him by having another man's baby. Have you ever been betrayed by a loved one? By a friend? How did you deal with it? Were you able to forgive them?

9. Both Laura and Sean felt guilty because Stephen had killed himself. They had thought they could have done something to change that. Blame can be devastating to a person. Has guilt ever affected you? How did you get over it? Did your faith help you work your way through the guilt?

10. God's plans for us aren't always the same as ours. Peter had always wanted to be a father, but he discovered he couldn't have children. Have you ever wanted something badly and couldn't have it? What did you do about it? Did your faith help you or did you turn away from the Lord?

REQUEST YOUR FREE BOOKS!

2 FREE INSPIRATIONAL NOVELS
PLUS 2
FREE
MYSTERY GIFTS

LoveInspired.

YES! Please send me 2 FREE Love Inspired® novels and my 2 FREE mystery gifts. After receiving them, if I don't wish to receive any more books, I can return the shipping statement marked "cancel." If I don't cancel, I will receive 4 brand-new novels every month and be billed just $3.99 per book in the U.S., or $4.74 per book in Canada, plus 25¢ shipping and handling per book and applicable taxes, if any*. That's a savings of 20% off the cover price! I understand that accepting the 2 free books and gifts places me under no obligation to buy anything. I can always return a shipment and cancel at any time. Even if I never buy another book from Steeple Hill, the two free books and gifts are mine to keep forever.

113 IDN EF26 313 IDN EF27

Name	(PLEASE PRINT)

Address	Apt. #

City	State/Prov.	Zip/Postal Code

Signature (if under 18, a parent or guardian must sign)

Order online at www.LoveInspiredBooks.com

Or mail to Steeple Hill Reader Service™:

IN U.S.A.: P.O. Box 1867, Buffalo, NY 14240-1867
IN CANADA: P.O. Box 609, Fort Erie, Ontario L2A 5X3

Not valid to current Love Inspired subscribers.

Want to try two free books from another series?
Call 1-800-873-8635 or visit www.morefreebooks.com

* Terms and prices subject to change without notice. NY residents add applicable sales tax. Canadian residents will be charged applicable provincial taxes and GST. This offer is limited to one order per household. All orders subject to approval. Credit or debit balances in a customer's account(s) may be offset by any other outstanding balance owed by or to the customer. Please allow 4 to 6 weeks for delivery.

Your Privacy: Steeple Hill is committed to protecting your privacy. Our Privacy Policy is available online at www.eHarlequin.com or upon request from the Reader Service. From time to time we make our lists of customers available to reputable firms who may have a product or service of interest to you. If you would prefer we not share your name and address, please check here. ☐

LIREG07

TITLES AVAILABLE NEXT MONTH

Don't miss these four stories in May

TO LOVE AGAIN by Bonnie K. Winn
A Rosewood, Texas novel

Laura Manning moved her family to Rosewood to take over her late husband's share of a real-estate firm. Who was Paul Russell to tell her she couldn't? She'd prove to the handsome Texan that she could do anything.

A SOLDIER'S HEART by Marta Perry
The Flanagans

After wounded army officer Luke Marino was sent home, he refused physical therapy. But Mary Kate Flanagan Donnelly needed Luke's case to prove herself a capable therapist. If only it wasn't so hard to keep matters strictly business...

MOM IN THE MIDDLE by Mae Nunn
Texas Treasures

Juggling caring for her son and elderly parents kept widow Abby Cramer busy. Then her mother broke her hip at a store. Good thing store employee Guy Hardy rushed in to save the day with his tender kindness toward her whole family—especially Abby herself.

HOME SWEET TEXAS by Sharon Gillenwater

When a strange man appeared to her like a mirage in the desert, he was the answer to the lost and injured woman's prayers. But she couldn't tell her handsome rescuer, Jake Trayner, who she was. Because she couldn't remember....

LICNM0407